'Til We Meet Again

Pamela Griffin

Heartsong Presents

Thank you to my entire family for their love, encouragement, and support. In particular I wish to thank my "editor mother" and "computer genius father," Arlene and John Trampel; and Lena Dooley, for her patience and mentoring.

And thank you, Brandon and Joshua, for being patient when Mommy was on the computer so often. I love you both!

I also wish to thank Philip Hind for his permission to use the wealth of information I gleaned from his web site.

But most of all, a special thank-you goes to the Master Storyteller, without whom this book would not have been written. It is to the Lord that I dedicate *'Til We Meet Again.*

A note from the author:
I love to hear from my readers! You may correspond with me by writing:

Pamela Griffin
Author Relations
PO Box 719
Uhrichsville, OH 44683

ISBN 1-57748-758-3

'TIL WE MEET AGAIN

Cover illustration by Ron Hall.

PRINTED IN THE U.S.A.

one

1912

A teasing breeze played with Annabelle's dark curls as she stood on the sun-splashed deck of the eleven-story ocean liner and watched the activity all around her.

She didn't look over the white balustrade toward the bustling English town below. Nor did she watch the pale-skinned, rosy-cheeked children as they gazed up in awe at the huge ship readying to depart from port. And she didn't pay attention to the few photographers and reporters on the wharf, snapping their black box cameras or writing furiously in their small notepads.

Annabelle Mooreland had had enough of the town of Southampton—all of England, for that matter—and she was anxious to leave. She had especially had enough of a certain Englishman who'd pulled the wool over her eyes.

Feeling terribly naïve and stupid, Annabelle grimaced. A hint of pink tinged her creamy skin when she thought of Roger Fieldhall. Best not to think about his kind or she might cry or scream or do something else embarrassing; she certainly didn't want that.

She tilted her head and, shielding her eyes from the brilliant sunshine with one hand, watched as a huge wooden crate was hoisted upward with ropes and pulleys; it swung past one of the towering smokestacks and was stowed in the hold of the ship. All around her, hundreds of well-dressed people stood and waved to those on land, many of them oblivious to the preparations taking place behind them.

Ladies wearing linen and silk day dresses and enormous wide-brimmed hats and men dressed just as extravagantly in silk and serge suits and wearing bowlers on their heads stood along the railing, strolled the decks, and investigated their home for the next week. Still others went below, seeking out their rooms.

One family had one of those new cameras that took moving pictures. It sat on a rickety-looking tripod, the man behind it winding the crank at the side and filming the day's events.

Annabelle noticed a distinguished-looking, silver-haired gentleman wearing leather gloves and carrying a gold-topped walking stick. Briefly she wondered how her father was faring. Totally unaffected by this milestone event in ocean travel in which he was playing a small part simply by being a passenger, he had retired to the men's smoking lounge to smoke his pipe and talk politics with anyone who would listen.

Annabelle sighed. She loved her father but hated the rank smell of his pipe—even though the tobacco was imported and some of the most expensive to be found, as her father had told her countless times. In deference to his daughter's "delicate smelling apparatus," as he teasingly called her nose, he had agreed to remove his "smelly old pipe" from her company. But his twinkling eyes had shown her he wasn't one bit angry.

Annabelle knew that in his blustering, awkward way, her father was simply giving her time to come to terms with her broken engagement. He'd never before demonstrated the slightest concern about smoking in her presence, but the reserved Englishman obviously recognized his daughter's need to spend time alone now.

Skirting knots of excited passengers, Annabelle escaped the noisy crowd and pulled her short, fitted jacket closer around her waist. She walked past the wooden lifeboats to the other, less-populated side of the ship that faced the sparkling ocean.

Actually, she would have appreciated a hug before her father left. But he'd never been the demonstrative type. As a child, Annabelle used to wonder why her American-born mother—a spirited, fiery woman—had married the staid Englishman. However, as she grew older, Annabelle learned to appreciate her father's hidden qualities. Although he hadn't mentioned the fight she'd had with Roger, her father had been sensitive enough to realize Annabelle was hurting.

Again Annabelle flushed with humiliation.

She should have known the dashing, young yet penniless Roger Fieldhall—famous polo player—had only been interested in her for her father's money. Though Annabelle assumed she was rather pretty from what her reflection in the mirror revealed, she knew her looks weren't anything spectacular. And while her personality was agreeable, she wasn't charming and flirtatious—not like the blond, delicate Mary Flossman, in whose arms Annabelle had found Roger upon her surprise visit to the stables a week ago.

She clenched her teeth, trying to maintain her composure, and again berated herself for her folly. Her friend Patricia had often told her she would be a fool to marry someone who didn't share her faith. At least Annabelle had discovered the truth of that statement before it was too late. She knew she'd been wrong to get closely involved with a non-Christian; but for the most part, hers had been a lonely life, and the possibility of spending her future as an old maid had no appeal. When Roger had proposed a year ago and offered Annabelle a part in his exciting life of fame, she quickly agreed—though she didn't love him. Only one man had ever held the key to her heart.

Annabelle impatiently flicked a tear away. No. She mustn't think about him, either. It had been four long years since she'd last seen him, and now he was promised to another.

Sighing, Annabelle tightly clasped her hands, forcing herself to concentrate on something else as she watched a gull soar and dive over the sparkling water.

When he'd seen how upset she was, her father had decided to leave for the States months sooner than originally planned and take Annabelle with him. He'd made the last-minute arrangements quickly and easily. Indeed, it seemed that when one had money, all manner of things were possible—even obtaining first-class cabins aboard a luxury ocean liner a day before departure and another in second class for Annabelle's maid, Sadie.

Annabelle knew she should be looking forward to this voyage, as Patricia had so enviously told her. But she wasn't.

Lord, is it my lot in life to be alone? Is there nothing else for me? She stepped back from the rail, intent on seeking out her stateroom.

A small blue-and-gold object suddenly came hurtling toward Annabelle, striking her and almost knocking her down.

"Oh, my!" Annabelle teetered backward, grabbed the rail, and regained her balance. She reached up and straightened her broad-brimmed, gaily beribboned hat, which had been knocked slightly askew. A small pink and white face, with two of the bluest eyes—like cornflowers—turned upward.

"I'm sorry," murmured the little girl, who looked to be no more than five, as she backed a step away. "I have to fin' my dolly."

Annabelle knelt down to the child's level. "What's your name, sweetheart? And where's your mommy?"

From under the soft round hat a cascade of blond curls swished over the navy-blue wool coat as the child shook her head back and forth. "Not s'posed to talk to strangers."

Annabelle bit the inside of her lower lip and looked around the deck, hoping to find an anxious face searching for a child. An olive-skinned, black-haired woman with fearful dark eyes caught sight of Annabelle and the little girl from about twenty yards away. Her face relaxed as she walked quickly toward them. Annabelle studied the woman curiously and then the fair child. The stranger certainly couldn't be the little girl's mother. They weren't a bit alike.

"Missy! You must never run off like that again," the woman said breathlessly with a Spanish accent. "If your mother knew what you did, she would be worried. *Si?"*

Chastened, Missy nodded. "But what about Helena?"

"She was probably packed with the luggage by mistake. I am certain when we reach our cabin, she will be there."

The woman seemed to notice Annabelle for the first time. Though her manner wasn't unfriendly, it became very reserved. "I wish to thank you for your help. If you had not stopped her when you did, Missy may have left the boat. *Gracias."*

Annabelle smiled and glanced at the little girl. "Well, I can't take all the credit. Actually. . ." Missy's big blue eyes cut quickly to hers, silently begging her not to tell of the near mishap. "I was glad to help," Annabelle quickly ended.

The woman nodded, though her expression was curious.

After a grateful smile to Annabelle, Missy turned to her companion. "Maria, do you really think Helena's in my trunk?"

Instantly a gentle look touched the dark eyes. *"Si,* little *señorita.* Perhaps we should go look now—yes?"

Missy nodded, then looked at Annabelle. "What's your name?"

"Annabelle."

"Ooooh. I like that," Missy trilled. "I want to name my next dolly that." Her fine brows raised. "Are you a stranger?"

Annabelle quickly glanced at the reserved Maria, who looked on silently, then back to Missy. "Yes, Missy. I suppose I am."

The little girl looked puzzled. "But how can you be a stranger if we know each other's names?"

Annabelle was flustered. She didn't know how to deal with children. She'd never had any brothers or sisters—none that she remembered anyway. Her older sister had died in a sledding accident when Annabelle had been only four, and her baby brother—born much too early—had died a few hours after his birth.

Maria took over and reached for the child's hand. "Come,

Missy. Perhaps, we will see Miss Annabelle again during the voyage, and you can talk to her then, hmmm? We must go now."

Annabelle watched them walk away. Missy looked over her shoulder and smiled. Annabelle smiled back. What a delightful little girl! Though Annabelle had little experience conversing with children, she looked forward to talking to Missy again. That is, if her nanny, or nursemaid, or whatever the exotic-looking Spanish woman was to the child, would let her.

Maria was a mystery. Her fine clothes spoke of wealth—definitely not something a domestic would wear—and her voice had been well modulated. As Annabelle looked back at the silver-tipped water, she wondered about her two new acquaintances. . . .

❧

On the pretext of studying the ocean, Lawrence casually leaned against the rail and looked instead at the pretty young woman standing several yards away. She was modestly outfitted in a long, pinstriped traveling dress and matching jacket. There was something familiar about her face—what he could see of it.

He searched his mind trying to place her but came up empty. Perhaps she'd been one of the many guests at his mother's soirees and balls in past years. He'd attended such functions only because it was required of a viscount, but he had always made excuses to leave at the first opportunity, wishing to evade the simpering young ladies who always sought him out. But this woman didn't look like one of their kind. There was a sweet innocence about her that enchanted him.

His eyes narrowed when he saw her flick away another tear. She'd been silently crying before the little girl had run into her, too, so he knew the collision hadn't caused the tears.

Was she married? Lawrence wished he could see her hand, but she was wringing both of them, her forearms lightly resting on the rail in front of her. He watched as she hastily lifted an arm and clutched the top of her straw hat when a sudden gust of April wind mussed her dark curls.

His heart lightened. No band of gold shimmered on her left hand, which he could now see clearly.

Lawrence wished he had the courage to approach her; but that kind of thing simply wasn't done, as far as he was concerned. Though in this day and age, he noted, many of his peers didn't have the gracious manners that had been instilled in Lawrence by two very proper English parents. Some men might not consider it too forward to talk to the pretty woman without benefit of an introduction—especially since she seemed so familiar. . . . But no, he couldn't do it.

Sometimes Lawrence felt as if he should have been born in an earlier time—a time when honor and chivalry abounded and the young maidens were pure and innocent and sweet. Not money-hungry flirts like Frances.

His dark brows pulled down in a scowl, and he shifted his gaze to the rippling water. Frances had been more than willing for a marriage to take place between them, but Lawrence had always disliked her wild, uninhibited ways. Good thing, too, when he discovered the real reason for her interest.

Surprisingly, his father had agreed with his decision, although Lawrence hadn't told him everything concerning the fight he'd had with Frances the last time he'd seen her. Her father also was wealthy, and a marriage between her and Lawrence would join their lands in Fairhaven—a fact that Lord and Lady Caldwell had often pointed out to their son. But when Lawrence firmly told them he couldn't marry her, his father had offered little objection.

Even more astounding to Lawrence was the fact that his father hadn't been against his taking this voyage. He had told Lawrence that perhaps once he had seen some of the world he would be ready to settle down and live the life of a nobleman in the Caldwells' sprawling Tudor manor.

Though Lawrence loved his homeland and knew he must return one day, he doubted it would be anytime soon. The thirst for adventure was strong in his blood. He wondered if one of his ancestors might have been a daring adventurer, such as a captain on the high seas or perhaps a buccaneer or a swashbuckler accomplished with the sword and always at the ready to rescue fair maidens. Lawrence often likened himself to the fictitious Sir Lancelot because he shared the famous knight's name—Lancelot being Lawrence's middle name. But where was *his* Guinevere? Had she found and wed her Arthur?

With a deep sigh, he pushed away from the rail and whisked slender fingers through his dark hair. He was becoming entirely too fanciful. No. . .more like ridiculous. Ever since this past winter, when he turned twenty-five, he'd given more thought to the idea of marriage. But if he were honest with himself, he'd have to admit he probably never would have married Frances, despite his parents' wishes. She wasn't his type. And her unscrupulous behavior had given him the reason he needed to terminate the relationship.

He turned toward the woman and hesitated, watching as the salty wet wind played against her, molding her linen dress to her slender figure and whipping tendrils of black curls about her rosy face. *Why does she seem so familiar?*

The question bothered him to no end, and, almost as though his foot had taken on a life of its own, Lawrence took a step in her direction, then stopped, suddenly realizing what he was doing. Forcing himself to turn away, he shoved his hands deep into the pockets of his overcoat, dodged several fellow passengers, and walked to the first-class companionway in search of his room.

❧

Once the tall gentleman moved away from the rail, Annabelle relaxed, letting a soft sigh of relief escape her lips. She'd been more than a little aware of the frequent glances he'd cast in her direction and was glad to see him go. She hadn't taken a good look at him while he'd been watching her, for to turn and stare back would have been considered much too bold, not to mention highly embarrassing. But now it was her turn to watch.

Annabelle easily picked out his tall, slender form in the charcoal-gray overcoat as he wove his way among the people strolling along the boat deck. Suddenly he stopped and picked up a reticule a middle-aged woman had dropped, turning sideways and doffing his bowler hat courteously as he returned it to her.

Annabelle's eyes widened and her heart gave a little flip as the years rolled back and she was a young girl in her uncle's house once again. *No. . .it couldn't be!*

Clutching the rail for support, she studied him in disbelief, noting his handsome profile, his gracious smile to the woman—who was now all a-dither, her face beaming. Though his shoulders weren't broad, his carriage was commanding, erect. He looked strong, capable, and dependable, much like. . .but that was impossible! *He* was a Caldwell—heir to the family title and a vast fortune. What would he be doing embarking on this voyage?

It had to be someone who strongly resembled him. Yes, of course that was it. Her brief thoughts of him earlier must have caused her to see his face in that of a stranger.

Annabelle's frantic pulse rate slowed to normal, and she relaxed her tight grip on the rail. Idly studying the retreating figure a moment longer, she almost jumped when an ear-splitting blast from the ship's whistle signaled it was time to depart.

Not wanting to join in the festivities, Annabelle hurried to the deck below, escaping the excited shouts and cheers of other passengers, who stood at the rail and watched as the *S.S. Titanic* slipped away from the dock, ready to embark on her maiden voyage.

two

Annabelle pulled a long, gold-trimmed evening gown with short sleeves from her trunk. She slipped it on, fastening it in back with only a little difficulty. It took longer to dress without Sadie there, but Annabelle managed. She finished by pulling on a pair of long white gloves. Looking into the mirror mounted onto the carved dresser, she critically studied her reflection.

The soft material of the gown gently molded her upper body, then fell in a straight line to her matching satin pumps. The color was the exact hue of her eyes—what Annabelle felt to be her one outstanding feature. She wore her mother's emerald pendant and matching earrings, and she'd swept her hair up off her neck and pinned it to the back of her head in what she hoped passed for an elegant style.

Annabelle walked to the curtained porthole and looked out at the black ocean below, at the twinkling stars and hazy moon in the nighttime sky. Bright yellow splashes of light from hundreds of portholes and windows along the ship shimmered on the dark water beneath her. Perhaps after dinner she would take a walk along the promenade and enjoy the beautiful evening. However, it did seem a lonely thing to do without someone by her side. A pair of ice-blue eyes in a handsome face came to mind. She hadn't been able to stop thinking about *him* since she'd mistaken that stranger for him earlier today.

With a disgusted sigh, she hurriedly turned from the romantic view. Rifling through her jewelry box, she plucked out a green rhinestone comb and slid it over lustrous black curls now contained in a French twist. Or rather, what she hoped passed for a French twist. She didn't have a lot of experience when it came to fixing her hair. At least her curls were natural, the one thing she'd inherited from her English grandmother. And the salt air seemed to give the ringlets even more bounce, Annabelle noted as she pulled away tiny tendrils with her comb, allowing them to dance about her face and neck when she moved.

Her maid had been sick upon boarding, and Annabelle had told her to stay in her room until she recovered. Annabelle remembered being seasick on the voyage to England eight years ago. But that couldn't be Sadie's problem; the ocean was calm.

A light knock sounded on her stateroom door. Annabelle put down the silver-plated comb, took one last look in the mirror, then walked across the cream-colored carpet to join her father.

❧

When the door opened and Edward Mooreland saw his daughter standing there, he tensed. It was amazing how much she reminded him of Cynthia—Annabelle's mother—who had died years ago. Though Cynthia's hair had been straight and the color a deep russet, the emerald eyes looking up at him from beneath thick, dark lashes and the sweet smile on his daughter's rosy lips were the same as her mother's.

Lately, now that Annabelle was maturing into a young woman, Edward noticed that his daughter resembled Cynthia more and more with each passing day. It hurt him to look at Annabelle or be in her company, though he was ashamed to admit it. Even eight years after losing Cynthia, the pain was there, sharpened when he looked upon her likeness.

Annabelle took his arm, noting its stiffness, and glanced up at him. He gave her a shaky smile before looking away.

❧

As they silently walked down the carpeted corridor to the lifts that would take them to D-deck, where the first-class dining room was located, Annabelle again sent a prayer heavenward, asking God to heal the breach between her and her father.

Upon entering the luxurious dining area, Annabelle inhaled softly, her eyes opening wide in wonder. The accommodations were magnificent! Carved white pillars, towering from floor to ceiling, stood sentinel throughout the spacious room, and tables of various sizes were grouped all across the brightly patterned linoleum. Covered with pristine white cloths, matching napkins, patterned china, crystal glasses, and silver utensils, they appealed to the eye, beckoning the people to come and dine. From one side of the oak-paneled room a band softly played music for the dinner patrons, who were rapidly filling the area.

A black-coated waiter led Annabelle and her father to one of the tables near the middle of the room. Those they would eat with had not yet arrived, and so for now, Annabelle and her father had the table to themselves. The waiter pulled out one of eight cushioned, red leather chairs, arranged around the table in twos, and she sat down and thanked him. After taking their orders for the first course, he bowed graciously, then left.

Annabelle turned to face her father, who'd been seated next to her, and voiced something that had been on her mind since they'd left Southampton. "Father, doesn't it bother you that the *Titanic* has never sailed before this voyage? I mean, it's all quite elegant, but this is her first time out to sea—the ship is completely new! I even noticed several painters disembarking before we left the pier, obviously having just completed their job, judging from the fresh smell of paint in the corridor."

"Annabelle, you worry too much," he gruffly reassured her. "Several men I've recently met told me she is virtually unsinkable. In fact, of all the ocean liners we could have chosen, the *Titanic* is by far the safest." He gave her a smile, and she relaxed a bit.

"Earlier today I met a gentleman by the name of Thomas Andrews," he said. "Incidentally, he oversaw the construction of this ship, and I heard him reassure another gentleman—who had questions similar to yours—of the absolute seaworthiness of her. Why, are you aware the *Titanic* is four city blocks long and took three years to build?" he added, obviously awed by the information. She shook her head, and he continued. "Captain Smith has been with the White Star Line for twenty-five years and has an outstanding record with them. I've heard this is his last voyage before retirement. So you've nothing at all to fear, my dear. You're in good hands."

Annabelle nodded, though she still wasn't thoroughly convinced. Yes, she'd seen a demonstration of the Captain's prowess when, upon leaving the waters of Southampton, a collision with a steamer called the *New York* had narrowly been avoided. In horror she'd stood at her porthole and watched as the small steamer had come closer and closer to the black hull of the *Titanic*. However, Captain Smith had somehow managed to avoid a collision. Still, to Annabelle's way of thinking, it hadn't been a great way to start an ocean voyage.

Forcing herself to stop her musings, Annabelle lifted her glass to her lips and stared out over the bustling dining room. Studying the elegant decor, she turned her head and watched as a well-dressed man approached their table. The small smile froze on her lips. Her mouth went dry as she stared in shock and realized the impossible was indeed possible.

The newcomer briefly looked at her fixed gaze a little oddly, but gave a polite nod. Then he saw her father. "Mr. Mooreland, I believe?" he asked in that rich, cultured voice she loved so well.

Edward broke into a smile. "Lord Caldwell, as I live and breathe! Sit down, sit down. You remember my daughter?"

Lawrence stiffened, his ice-blue eyes going wide as he turned his head to look her way again. "Annabelle?" he murmured in shock, as he slowly sank to the chair on her right, never taking his searching eyes from her face. "Is it really you?"

At her hesitant nod, he continued. "I sincerely doubt I

would have recognized you had it not been for your father."

She gave a nervous laugh. "Considering I was in pigtails and pinafores at the time, I wouldn't wonder." She twisted the linen napkin in her lap, hardly daring to believe this was really happening. The love of her life was here, on board the *Titanic*, sitting next to her!

"How long has it been?" Lawrence asked, his voice soft.

"Four years."

"Four years. . . ," he repeated, his words trailing away. Annabelle swallowed, staring into his beautiful eyes. The contrast between them and his coal-black lashes and dark brows made them appear like ice—though the expression in them was very warm.

"It's lovely to see you again, Lord Caldwell," she managed.

"Please, Annabelle, cease the formalities. Considering the friendship we shared, to you I'll always be Lawrence."

His words warmed her, but further conversation was halted as a waiter appeared at their table, an elderly couple trailing behind. They took their seats across from Annabelle and her father and introduced themselves as Mr. and Mrs. Isidor Straus. Less than a minute later, the last couple waltzed in and took their places at the table.

Annabelle inwardly cringed when she saw the young woman. She had heavily rouged cheeks and lips and hair the color of fire. A cocoa-colored gown covered her hourglass figure, and a matching feathered plume waved from the top of her piled-up curls. Annabelle was shocked at the woman's low-scooped neckline, which clearly exposed a bit too much flesh, to her way of thinking. Judging from Mrs. Straus's horrified reaction, she, too, thought the woman was dressed inappropriately for the occasion.

The man—also flamboyantly attired—sat down beside her at the other end of the table, facing Lawrence. He introduced himself as Eric Fontaneau and the woman as his sister, Charlotte.

Annabelle took an instant dislike to her. She was too much of a flirt, as evidenced by the shameless way she leaned across the table and spoke to Lawrence during the meal. Much to his credit, he barely gave anything more than a polite reply to her questions and didn't stare at her as many of the other men in the dining room were doing. But then, he'd always been a perfect gentleman. It was one of the things Annabelle loved about him.

The memory of a shy eleven-year-old peering through the banister rails at a ballroom full of splendidly dressed dancers came to Annabelle's mind. She had sat huddled on the carpeted stairs, her bare toes peeked out from beneath her long cotton nightgown and wrapper, and tried to stay hidden, hoping her absence from the bedroom wouldn't be discovered. Feeling as if someone were watching her, she had looked sideways toward the bottom of the stairs and had spotted Lawrence leaning against the wall.

At first she'd been awed by the tall, handsome young viscount whom she'd admired from afar, as well as a little fearful he would angrily demand to know what she was doing there and send for her nanny. Being out of bed past midnight and spying on the guests would've gotten Annabelle into trouble with her strict uncle, whom she and her father were living with at the time.

But Lawrence had neither yelled nor gone for assistance. Instead, he walked up the stairs and sat next to her. "Hello," he said softly. "You must be Annabelle." At her slight nod, he offered a friendly handshake and smile. "I'm Lawrence."

To her amazement he had spent the next few minutes conversing with her, harmlessly joking about several guests dancing below them and making Annabelle laugh—something she hadn't done in a long time. It was then that her little girl heart began to see him as special. The fact that someone so handsome, so sought after by the pretty girls at the dance, would leave the party and spend time with her, a mere child, endeared Lawrence to Annabelle, making him a hero in her eyes.

Because her uncle and Lawrence's father were good friends, the families got together often, and each time she saw Lawrence, he made a point to spend time with her—talking with and reading to her, riding horses with her, and sometimes helping her with her studies. He treated her special—always seeming to care about what she had to say and how she felt—and a strong friendship developed between them, a closeness which, for Annabelle, had led to love. But Lawrence had never known of her strong feelings for him; it was a secret she'd closely guarded in her heart.

A waiter came with the third course of poached salmon in mousseline sauce, and Annabelle hastily took a helping, realizing with embarrassment that she'd been openly staring at Lawrence. He probably hadn't noticed, though, since he was discussing business with Mr. Straus, cofounder of Macy's in New York.

She took a few tiny bites, then turned her head and noted with dismay that Charlotte's interests were now focused on her father. And he didn't seem to be dissuading her, either.

"I miss the freckles," Lawrence said softly for Annabelle's ears alone.

She turned to him, startled, certain she'd heard wrong. Her stomach did a little flip when she met his eyes. "What?"

"Your freckles. I miss them."

Embarrassed, she blushed, her lashes briefly flicking downward. "I lost most of them when I turned seventeen two years ago. I'll soon be nineteen, you know," she said a little shyly.

"Nineteen. . . ," he said with a teasing grin. "Why, it seems like only yesterday you were romping over the grounds at Fairview Manor and begging to ride Thunder."

She frowned at him. "I never romped. Romping is for boys. I skipped."

He gave an easy laugh, his eyes crinkling at the corners. "Ah, Annabelle. You always were such a delightful child."

Something clutched at her heart. *"A delightful child."* And did he still see her as a child? Did he still equate her with the freckle-faced urchin with a cloud of unruly dark hair who had often come to the Caldwells' stables to ride the horses? *Oh,*

Lawrence, open your eyes—I'm a woman now!

But it didn't really matter what he thought, she supposed, feeling a hint of despair. He loved another. Idly she wondered how Frances felt about Lawrence taking a voyage to America.

A lilting laugh sounded across the table. Annabelle looked at Charlotte, who was talking to her father. His cheeks went ruddy, and he gave the woman next to him a grin. What could that painted woman have said to make her staid father react like that?

Distressed by his unusual behavior and disappointed that Lawrence still thought her a child, Annabelle somehow managed to sit through the next five courses, eating little of what the waiters offered on their silver salvers.

Foregoing dessert, she pleaded a headache, and her father excused himself and turned to her, offering assistance. To Annabelle's dismay, the Fontaneaus also rose, claiming they, too, were ready to depart. It helped that Lawrence accompanied them, but when Annabelle discovered that the Fontaneaus' rooms were on the same corridor as her and her father's rooms, she softly groaned.

Upon reaching her door, Annabelle said good night, stressing the word when she said it to her father. He didn't appear to notice, but nodded and gave a cheery "Good night, Annabelle." But Lawrence seemed to notice.

"I hope you soon feel better," he said softly. He gave her arm a squeeze before dropping it, showing he understood, and she offered a weak smile in return, thankful for his consideration and support. At least she still had his friendship.

Before Annabelle closed the door on the retreating figures, she saw Charlotte take her father's arm and smile, fluttering her long, dark lashes. In disbelief Annabelle watched as the woman sidled up to him, steering him away from his room and toward the grand staircase. Annabelle just managed not to slam her door.

Turning, she looked at the cheery pink and blue furnishings, the delicate Queen Anne furniture, the white marble fireplace—and she wanted to scream. Sinking onto the plush blue sofa, she plucked up one of the round pink cushions, clutching it to her breast.

"Lord, how can Father not see what type of woman she is? If that French accent is real, I'll, I'll. . ." Annabelle looked around the room. "I'll trade in this luxurious stateroom for one of the third-class rooms in steerage!" She threw the pillow down. "And that can't be the natural color of her hair; no woman has hair that color! Why, Mama was ten times prettier than Charlotte Fontaneau, and that's the truth!"

The words stabbed like a knife blade to the heart, and her eyes closed. Was Annabelle jealous of the interest her father was showing Charlotte because Annabelle thought he was wronging her mother's memory in some way. . .or was she jealous of the attention he gave the woman because he rarely showed any interest in his own daughter? Her eyes opened wide at this new thought, and she silently admitted the latter.

With only the care of a stern uncle, a distant father, and an aunt who had "more important matters to take care of than spending time with a runny-nosed child," it was small wonder Annabelle had clung to the sweet friendship she'd shared with Lawrence while growing up.

And she must learn to be satisfied with *only* friendship, she reminded herself yet again. Frances was the woman he loved.

Sighing, she rose from the couch and changed into a white, ruffled nightgown. Then, grabbing her Bible, she climbed onto the soft mattress. But she was too upset to concentrate on nightly devotions. Laying the Bible on a nearby chair, Annabelle stared at the electric fireplace that took the chill out of the room.

Unfortunately, it did nothing to take the chill out of her heart.

three

Before dawn the next morning, Lawrence rose from bed, groomed, and hurriedly dressed. He wanted to take advantage of the ship's gymnasium. A believer in the value of physical fitness, Lawrence almost took it to the extreme. Horseback riding, fencing, canoeing, lifting weights—he'd enjoyed all of these at Fairview, his ancestral home, and he was anxious to see what the *Titanic* provided for the athlete.

He walked up the stairs to the boat deck, easily finding the large gymnasium. Making his way toward a rowing machine, Lawrence again thought of Annabelle. He still found it hard to believe she was the woman he'd been staring at before they'd left Southampton. He remembered last night, how she'd shyly told him she was approaching her nineteenth birthday. Annabelle Mooreland. . .a young woman. Unbelievable.

He thought about when he'd first seen her at Mooreland Hall—a little waif cowering on the stairs during the Harvest Ball, afraid of being discovered. His mother had told him Annabelle had recently sailed to England with her father, having lost her mother several months prior to the voyage. He had seen the pain and uncertainty in her wide emerald eyes and pinched white face and had made an effort to befriend the lonely little girl. His kindness had been prompted by sympathy, but as Lawrence got to know her, he'd thoroughly enjoyed the independent little miss—her feistiness, her sweetness, her innocence—and had treated her like the younger sister he'd never had.

However, the feelings that had raced through him upon seeing her again were *not* those one would feel for a younger sibling. Ridiculous! He was six years older than she was; at her age, she probably thought him an old man. Still, he would like to renew their friendship, if she were agreeable. . . .

The muscles of his chest strained against the thin material of his shirt, and his strong arms glistened with sweat as he pulled on the oars of the rowing machine with steady strokes. After about ten minutes of rigorous exercise, Lawrence mounted one of the mechanical bicycles and gave his legs a good workout. He lifted a few weights, then rolled down his sleeves, shrugged into his coat, and headed for the freshwater bathing pool, Annabelle on his mind the whole time.

❧

"Good morning."

Annabelle looked up from her book, shocked to see Lawrence standing there. He smiled and motioned to the empty chair next to her. "May I?"

Eyes wide, she nodded.

"I missed you at breakfast," Lawrence said softly as he sat down and faced her. "Your father said you still weren't feeling well. I hope you're much improved now?"

Her heart fluttered. Had he sought her out at breakfast? That's what his words implied. "Yes, I'm feeling much better. I had a small headache, but it's gone now. This wonderful salt air and sunshine are invigorating."

Lawrence nodded and took off his hat, pushing his fingers through his thick dark hair. "It's fortunate the ocean is so calm. Otherwise you might have to deal with being seasick—a most unpleasant sensation, from what I've heard."

"Yes, I know." Annabelle grimaced. "I remember having that problem on the journey to England eight years ago. And I believe my maid must be dealing with the same thing, though with the lovely weather conditions it does seem a bit strange. She's been sick since we boarded at Southampton."

"I'm sorry to hear that," Lawrence said sympathetically. "Is Mrs. Reardon still your maid?"

"Mrs. Reardon was my *nanny,*" Annabelle said, stressing the word. "I have a *ladies' maid* now. Father secured her services not long after I turned sixteen."

"A ladies' maid." He chuckled. "Let's hope you don't put frogs in *her* blankets before she retires for the evening," he teased, reminding her of an incident she'd once confidentially shared with him concerning her nanny.

Annabelle bristled. "Lawrence, really! I was twelve years old then. I'm not a child any longer!"

He straightened, the smile leaving his face. "Of course you're not. I was merely jesting, Annabelle. Please don't take offense." He looked away, wondering why she'd gotten so angry. Whenever he'd made such remarks in the past, he'd elicited a giggle out of her, which often turned into shared laughter between them. But the green eyes flashing at him now held no laughter.

After an uncomfortable silence, he looked down at the book in the lap of her dove-gray dress. "Might I ask what you're reading?" he said lightly.

She gave a faint smile, embarrassed to have reacted so crossly to his teasing comment. She realized he hadn't meant any harm by it. It wasn't in his nature to hurt someone's feelings. But oh, how she wished he would really look at her and see how she'd changed! "I visited the ship's library and found a copy of *The Pilgrim's Progress* by John Bunyan. Have you read it?"

"Ah, the adventures of Christian," Lawrence said, nodding. "An excellent book."

"Then you *have* read it?"

"Oh, yes. I think every Christian should read *The Pilgrim's Progress* to help enhance their spiritual journey."

Annabelle's heart soared. Roger had never wanted to discuss spiritual subjects, claiming they were much too deep and philosophical, and there were more exciting things in life to talk about. And Annabelle's father, though he'd once given his life to the Lord, rarely engaged in such discussions. Only with Lawrence had she been able to talk of spiritual matters.

"I like to think that when Christian arrived at the Celestial City," she said excitedly, "he prayed for Christiana, and through his prayers, she developed the desire to follow him and be saved."

Lawrence glanced out over the ocean and watched a gull dive over the sparkling water. He paused, considering. "An interesting concept. I'm not certain if there's Scripture to back up your theory, but I do know without a doubt that Jesus Christ is our personal intercessor to the Father."

She smiled, thrilled to discuss spiritual things with him again. She had so many questions, so many things she didn't know. The church she'd attended in Fairhaven was confusing and strangely empty, though it had been packed with the well-to-do of the area. "Does that mean, then, that we—those of us who are on the earth—aren't to intercede if Jesus is doing it for us already?" she asked, her words coming out a bit hasty in her excitement.

He looked startled by her question. "My word, no! Didn't the good Lord tell us how important it is to constantly be in prayer and thanksgiving and admonish us to pray for one another daily? Saint Paul also spoke of it in his many letters. I feel that if it weren't so important for us to take an active part in intercession—especially for the unsaved—then it wouldn't be referred to as often as it is throughout the Scriptures."

The morning passed quickly while they talked. The sun was directly overhead when they pulled into Queenstown, off the coast of Ireland, their last stop before heading out to sea.

Annabelle's hand flew to her mouth. "Oh, my! It must be close to noon," she exclaimed. "We've been talking for hours!"

Lawrence smiled warmly. "I can't think of any way I would prefer to spend the morning. I've enjoyed our conversation, Annabelle. I've missed them," he added softly. "That's one thing I would have liked to have had at Oxford—someone I could really open up to like I could with you. Oh, I had friends. . . . But with you it was different somehow."

She lowered her head, her cheeks warming. "I've missed you, too, Lawrence."

He smiled and held out his hand. "Would you care to take a turn around the deck with me, Annabelle? For old time's sake?"

She swallowed hard and nodded, allowing him to assist her. He replaced his hat, and she clutched the book to her breast as they began to stroll together along the sunny deck, reliving old memories and watching as hundreds of seagulls soared and dived in the *Titanic*'s wake.

❧

Annabelle stuck the end of the pen between her teeth, wondering what to write next in her letter to Patricia. She looked around the room at the other ladies, the Georgian-style furniture, the carved paneling, the exquisite décor of the light and airy reading and writing room—obviously designed for feminine tastes—and contemplated her dilemma.

Looking down at the ivory sheet of paper only half filled with flowery writing, she sighed. Should she tell Patricia about seeing Lawrence again? No, perhaps not. Annabelle had met Patricia at a banquet Annabelle had attended with Roger this past year, so Patricia didn't know Lawrence. And to tell her about him at this point would steal something away from the special friendship he and Annabelle shared. Her brow wrinkled.

Despite knowing Lawrence didn't have a romantic interest in her, it bothered Annabelle that he still thought her a child. Otherwise, wouldn't he have asked if she would like to visit the Café Parisian for tea and scones instead of inviting her for hot cocoa and macaroons? True, they'd been her favorites when she was a child, but she was a woman now! When would he see that?

Almost furiously, Annabelle began to write. A huge blob of black ink splotched the paper, entirely covering several of her words. "Oh, drat!" she fumed under her breath.

"Somethin' the matter, honey?"

Annabelle looked up at the handsome woman who sat across the table from her with a book in her hand. Bright blue eyes set in an oval face that spoke of strong character looked back at Annabelle. A cloud of dark reddish hair covered the woman's head—a gargantuan hat, loaded with flowers, covering it. Wearing a stiff navy blue dress with a white ruffled inset, the plump woman looked to be in her forties.

"I'm afraid I've ruined another sheet of stationery," Annabelle explained ruefully.

"Don't worry. I'm sure you can get another one. A ship like this one is bound to have plenty o' supplies."

Annabelle looked at the three crumpled pieces of paper at her elbow, the result of previous mistakes. "Yes, I know. . . it's not that. I simply don't seem to be able to focus on what I want to say right now." She sighed. "I suppose my mind is on other things."

"Your young man, for instance?"

Annabelle's head shot up at the woman's gentle query, and she looked across the table into laughing eyes.

"Forgive me if I'm a little too blunt, honey, but I couldn't help noticin' the two of you talkin' to each other this mornin' as I walked along the deck."

Annabelle blushed. "I notice you're an American," she said hastily to change the subject. "I, too, come from America—Manhattan, New York—though I've lived in England for the past eight years."

The woman nodded. "Newport's my home. Name's Mrs. Margaret Brown—but you can call me Maggie; everybody does." Her eyes twinkled. "You remind me of a young lady I met in Denver once—a sweet young thing. Met her not too long after James an' I met—that's my husband, you know, though now we're what people call 'estranged.' Strange word, isn't it? Strange—estranged. Get the connection?" She let out a loud laugh, eliciting disapproving stares from a few others in the room.

Annabelle was shocked at the boisterous behavior of the woman, though she thought she detected a look of sadness in the blue eyes and wondered if Mrs. Brown was really as indifferent concerning the situation with her husband as she appeared to be.

Maggie again took up the conversation but was stopped when the six o'clock bugle sounded the call that it was time to dress for dinner. They parted, Maggie issuing an invitation to get together for tea soon. Annabelle nodded vaguely and smiled.

At the moment, all she could think about was that soon she would see Lawrence again.

four

"Sadie, you should go back to your cabin. I don't think you're well enough to be up yet."

"I'll be all right, miss," the young blond quickly assured, though her tired hazel eyes belied her words. "At least let me do up your hair. I feel absolutely awful that you had to do it last night. And however did you manage your stays this morning?"

"I received help from a stewardess," Annabelle explained, fluffing her dress as she critically eyed her reflection in the mirror. "After you finish my hair I want you to go back to bed, though—and this time, I want you to stay there until you're one hundred percent better." She smiled at her maid. "Okay?"

Sadie nodded, and Annabelle sat down in a cushioned chair in front of the vanity, allowing Sadie to comb, weave, and sweep her hair up into an elaborate style, elegantly displaying her shining curls. Sadie was a skillful hairdresser, and Annabelle was secretly relieved for Sadie's expertise tonight. A jeweled hairpiece, sprinkled with tiny diamonds, provided the final touch as Sadie slipped it over Annabelle's head.

After Sadie left, Annabelle studied her reflection in the mirror. She wore a taupe-colored satin gown that shimmered in the light. The neckline was Grecian—gently gathered in shimmering ripples below the collarbone to fall in numerous folds down her back. Her mother's antique diamond pendant circled her neck, matching earrings dangled from her small ears, and long white gloves and satin pumps matching the gown completed the ensemble. Annabelle smiled at her reflection, satisfied. She hardly looked like a little girl now!

As she walked into the dining room on her father's arm and greeted other passengers she'd previously met, Annabelle glowed with the shocked look of approval and admiration

Lawrence gave her, and she was pleased she'd taken the extra effort with her preparations.

Even Charlotte's eyes opened wide. "Why, you look simply lovely, mademoiselle," she remarked, her green eyes taking full inventory of Annabelle. She turned to Edward, who sat beside her. "I can see where she gets her looks—*oui?*"

Edward's face turned ruddy, and Annabelle's mouth grew grim. Was it to be another night like last evening, with Charlotte fawning over her father the entire time?

Monsieur Fontaneau spoke up. "My sister speaks ze truth. You are truly a vision, mademoiselle. Perhaps you would care to accompany us to ze reception room after dinner? Your father has agreed to join us, so you will not go unchaperoned."

Annabelle looked to her father, but he ignored her. "I–I'm rather tired tonight, Monsieur Fontaneau, and directly after the meal I plan to retire to my stateroom to rest," she said quickly.

He nodded, but his ocean-deep blue eyes seemed to burn through her, demanding. . .what? Annabelle hastily looked away.

Lawrence watched the interchange between the two and a nerve ticked near his jaw. He didn't trust Eric Fontaneau one bit, whether he was the son of a French count—as Eric had told them last night—or not! And Lawrence certainly didn't want him around Annabelle. There was something about the man that seemed dangerous, phony—as if he were trying too hard to impress.

"Since your father has made other plans, I'd be more than happy to escort you to your stateroom after dinner, Annabelle," Lawrence said smoothly.

"A splendid idea, Lord Caldwell. So gracious of you to offer," Edward piped up immediately.

Lawrence's silver-blue eyes turned toward her. Eyes that reminded her of warm ice. Though the term was an odd one, it fit. His look seemed to melt her. "Annabelle?"

Annabelle nodded. "Thank you, Lawrence. I would like that very much."

The meal passed rather comfortably after that, except for one incident. Monsieur Fontaneau ordered a bottle of vintage wine, insisting everyone drink. Not willing to consume any form of alcohol, Annabelle declined and was pleased that Lawrence did likewise. But her father gladly accepted, much to Annabelle's dismay.

After the seventh course had been taken away and dessert served, Annabelle noted with disgust that Charlotte was now acting tipsy. True, wine, champagne, and liquor routinely flowed freely throughout the sumptuous meals—a waiter always at the ready to refill an empty glass—but tonight Mademoiselle Fontaneau seemed quite intoxicated. Had Annabelle imagined it or had Charlotte moved her chair closer to Annabelle's father's?

Annabelle angrily bit off the end of her chocolate éclair, wishing it was a certain woman's head. She forced herself to chew the cream-filled pastry, but when she was only halfway finished, she pushed her plate away and took a sip of water. Though *that* woman had ruined her dinner yet again, Annabelle refused to leave the table until everyone else did. She wouldn't go running off to her room like a silly child as she had done last night! She would show Lawrence she was a mature adult, capable of dealing with difficult situations.

Her heart sank when the waiter brought a bottle of champagne to the table at Charlotte's request.

Lawrence, seeming to sense her discomfort, said softly, "It's such a lovely evening. Shall we take a walk along the promenade before I escort you to your stateroom, Annabelle?"

A loud burst of laughter erupted from her father, and Annabelle turned her head, shocked. His whole being was focused upon Charlotte, who was speaking in husky, low tones, making it impossible for Annabelle to hear the words.

"I think I'll go now, Father. Lawrence has asked me to take a stroll with him before I retire for the night. Father! Did you hear what I said?"

"Hmmm?" Edward asked, turning to his daughter. His

eyes were dull, his expression dazed. "A walk, you say? Oh, yes—fine night for a walk. You might take a wrap, though. A bit chilly."

"*Good night,* Father."

❧

Lawrence wondered if he had been the only one who noticed the frosty tone of Annabelle's voice. Together they left the dining room. His hand on her elbow, they climbed the stairway to the next three levels and the covered promenade, which stretched out along the length of A-deck. They walked in silence, passing several couples strolling in the other direction.

"You don't like Mademoiselle Fontaneau, do you?" Lawrence asked thoughtfully, noting how Annabelle stiffened at the mention of the woman's name.

"Why do you say that?" She stopped and looked at him.

"Because of the way you react whenever she's in the vicinity. . .and speaks to your father."

"Speaks to him!" Annabelle blurted, her green eyes flashing fire. "*Throws* herself at him would be more accurate. The woman is nothing more than a cheap floozy dressed in satin and jewels!"

Her cheeks flushed and she turned her head away. "Forgive me, Lawrence. Father has often warned me that my tongue is my own worst enemy. I shouldn't have spoken so. You must think me without any refinement whatsoever," she said dully.

Lawrence smiled. "Think nothing of it. Now and then everyone speaks things better left unsaid."

"Really? Even you, Lawrence?" She looked up at him, her emerald eyes brilliant. Her back was to the calm ocean as they stood in front of one of the well-lit windows lining the deck. The bright light played over her features, emphasizing the soft curves of her cheeks and forehead, her lustrous curls, her rosy mouth.

Mentally he took a step backward, away from her, though his feet didn't move. "Perhaps we should continue our stroll now," he said, a bit gruffly.

Annabelle nodded, confused. This time he didn't take her arm when they continued to walk, and a pang went through her as she wondered what had made him so distant all of a sudden.

❧

Lawrence sat on the sofa in his stateroom, blankly staring at the intricately carved paneling on the brown walls. When he'd purchased his ticket, he'd chosen Italian Renaissance for his room from the variety of décor available to first-class passengers. He wondered what Annabelle's stateroom looked like. Probably something soft and feminine like her. . . .

"Lawrence Caldwell, stop this nonsense right now!" he ordered. "Six years' difference is a lifetime to someone her age." He chuckled dryly and whisked his fingers over the back of his hair. Now he was talking to himself.

Perhaps he should go to the smoking lounge and see if anyone was about. He didn't smoke but would rather seek out company there than sit all alone in this confining room with its dark furnishings and his depressing thoughts.

Lawrence left his stateroom, ascended the grand staircase, and walked down the corridor to the dimly lit smoking room. Upon entering, he saw Edward Mooreland sitting slumped over at a green, felt-topped table and strode across the carpet in that direction. He waited for the other man to notice him and finally cleared his throat. "Excuse me, Mr. Mooreland. I see that you're alone; would you mind if I join you, sir?"

Edward, eyes bleary, looked up from the brandy he was nursing between clutched hands. "Oh. Hello, Lord Caldwell. Alone?" he repeated wryly. "Yes, frightfully so." He looked down into his amber-colored drink.

Lawrence felt that Edward's enigmatic words went a lot deeper than the moment. Without invitation, he sat down in the dark brown leather chair across from Edward. The older man fiddled with his crystal brandy goblet, a grim expression on his face, then picked it up and downed the rest of the contents in one gulp. His hand shaking, he set it back on the table.

"Don't pay me any mind, my boy. I'm afraid I've had a turn of bad luck with the cards. Perhaps tomorrow night will prove more profitable." His eyes flicked upward. "Do you play?"

Lawrence shook his head, and Edward sighed. "I quit shortly after I met Cynthia—my wife," he explained. "However, Monsieur Fontaneau can be rather persuasive when it comes to the game, and I must admit, I was rather easy to persuade."

Lawrence's mouth narrowed to a straight line. Here was yet another reason not to like Eric Fontaneau. "I trust you didn't lose much." The statement was posed more as a question.

"A mere pittance." Edward waved a hand in dismissal, but Lawrence could clearly hear the undertone of anxiety in his voice.

"Then I'm glad, for your sake as well as your daughter's."

Edward's eyes misted. "Ah, Annabelle. She's a good girl." A small grin cracked his mouth below his trim mustache. "Though she's a bit spirited, like her mother was. Unfortunately, Annabelle has a habit of speaking her mind without considering the consequences. But I'm certain, after spending time in her company these past years, you've already found that to be the case."

"Actually, I find your daughter quite refreshing."

Something in Lawrence's tone alerted Edward, and he studied the younger man intently. "Annabelle is still a bit of a child, and though she will turn nineteen in a matter of weeks, she thinks like a little girl much of the time. Perhaps it's my fault. Perhaps I should have married so that she would have had a mother to raise her and teach her all the things a woman should know." Edward paused and cleared his throat before continuing. "It will take a strong man to take my daughter in hand. I know what a handful she can be."

"I don't think you have any reason to fear for Annabelle's future. Your daughter is a genuine lady. She doesn't hide the truth behind fluttering eyelashes and flirtatious speech, as do some of the women I've met," Lawrence said bitterly, thinking of Frances. "With Annabelle, a man knows what he will get."

Upon hearing Lawrence's quiet words, Edward flushed as a picture of Charlotte came to mind. "Don't be too certain of that! Perhaps you don't know her as well as you think. There's a lot more to Annabelle than meets the eye." He paused a moment, considering. "If I may be so bold, Lord Caldwell, do you have a personal reason for speaking thus?"

"I'm concerned for her welfare—nothing else," Lawrence said firmly. "She's always been dear to me, like my own sister."

Edward's eyes narrowed as he studied Lawrence, who seemed a bit too adamant, his eyes bright. Edward had a feeling the young man's interest went a lot further than he'd stated, whether he realized it or not, but Edward trusted him with Annabelle. He knew Lawrence's family well and had always been aware of the strong friendship between Lawrence and his daughter. In truth, he would have welcomed Lawrence as a son-in-law, but it was more important to Edward that his daughter find a man who truly loved her as he'd loved Cynthia. Especially after what that scoundrel Roger Fieldhall had done.

"Fair enough," Edward said, nodding.

Lawrence smoothed an imaginary crease from his black pant leg before speaking again. "Perhaps this is none of my business, Mr. Mooreland, but after our talk tonight, I feel I may be bold enough to discuss something else with you."

Edward inclined his head, his expression curious.

"Are you aware that Annabelle's behavior has been a bit, shall we say, strange lately?"

Instantly Edward's eyes flamed. "What do you mean by that remark, Lord Caldwell?" he demanded gruffly.

Lawrence paused, realizing he was going about this all wrong. "She's concerned for your welfare, sir."

"My welfare?" Edward exclaimed, incredulous.

"Yes." Lawrence looked him straight in the eye. "Your relationship with Mademoiselle Fontaneau has disturbed her greatly. Annabelle hasn't told me in so many words, but I detect that she's fearful your interest in the woman is deepening."

"Deepening?"

"As in marriage."

"Marriage!"

Upon hearing Edward's loud bellow, several of the other men in the room turned briefly to look toward their table. Edward straightened in his chair and lowered his voice. "I can't imagine why she would think such a thing! You must be mistaken."

"Perhaps. As I said, she didn't actually say it in so many words. I certainly don't expect you to confide in me, Mr. Mooreland, but since your wife died, have you paid as much attention to any other woman as you have to Mademoiselle Fontaneau?" *Including your own daughter,* he added silently, remembering how distant Edward had always been with Annabelle.

Edward's face turned ruddy, answering Lawrence's question.

"Perhaps you should talk with her," Lawrence suggested kindly. "It seems there's much that needs to be discussed between the two of you."

"Yes. Perhaps you're right," Edward tiredly conceded. "I'll talk to her tomorrow after breakfast."

five

Annabelle woke early and quickly dressed. Not bothering to wait for Sadie, she again secured a stewardess's help to lace her corset. After donning a pale green dress bearing a white-ribbed front and high collar, Annabelle attached a cameo to her throat—her father's birthday gift to her when she turned fourteen.

Loosely pinning up her hair, she studied her reflection in the oval mirror. Satisfied, she picked up her hat, then changed her mind and laid it back down. Not today. She wanted to feel the hot sun on her head and shoulders and allow the breeze to sift through her hair. She wished she could take it out of its confining pins. But, of course, that wouldn't be proper.

Excited with the approach of a new day, Annabelle left her room and walked down the corridor to ascend the magnificent grand staircase. Starting at the boat deck, the ship's uppermost level, dark, lacy wooden banisters and rails, which matched the color of the paneled walls, wrapped around the upper balcony in a semicircle and angled downward. At each end of the semicircle a short set of white stairs edged in gold led down to a small landing, then turned and widened into one long stairway that swept down, fanlike. On the wall in the middle of the landing, an intricate carving bore a clock in its center. A bronze statue of a cherub holding an electric torch stood on a pedestal at the end of the rail, at the bottom of the stairs. High above, a domed skylight shed a soft white glow on the room below.

To reach the next lower deck, one only had to do an about-face after descending the last stair, walk a few feet, and turn, where another flight of stairs led downward. The layout was the same on each level.

Annabelle lifted the hem of her dress with one hand and held on to the rail with the other, as she made her ascent to the boat deck. The ship also offered three passenger lifts, located opposite the stairway. Annabelle and her father had used the elevators when going to dinner the previous two nights, but this morning she preferred to walk.

Upon reaching her destination, Annabelle noted a chill in the air and was thankful she'd brought her thick shawl. Turning toward the stern of the boat, she gasped in awe at sight of the red disc of the sun just beginning to touch the sky and flood it with graceful ribbons of shimmering color. Annabelle walked toward the stern until she could go no farther. Clutching the rail, she stared, losing herself in the beautiful artwork of the Master Painter.

"Fantastic, isn't it?"

Startled, Annabelle turned and looked up into eyes that had always reminded her of warm ice. Her pulse rate increased when she saw how close he stood.

"Forgive me," Lawrence apologized softly. "I didn't mean to frighten you, Annabelle. I was going down to F-deck for a workout when I noticed you walking in this direction." He smiled. "I'd forgotten how you enjoyed early morning. . . . I remember when you and your family stayed at Fairview for several days after the Christmas party because a snowstorm made the roads hazardous—I was on break from university at the time. Do you remember, Annabelle?"

She nodded. How could she forget? It had been one of the last times she'd seen him. She'd just turned fifteen, a most awkward age, and had dressed and tiptoed down the stairs one morning to view the sunrise through the huge picture window facing east in the front parlor. When she noticed a light coming from the open door of the study, she panicked and quickly turned in flight. Stumbling, she caught her foot on the edge of the second stair and fell, ending up on her derrière in a most disgraceful manner, her gangly legs sprawled out in front of her.

Annabelle had been mortified when, upon hearing her soft cry, Lawrence hurried from the study and had seen her in the embarrassing position. But he hadn't said a word about her clumsiness; instead, he anxiously inquired if she were hurt.

When she shyly assured him she was all right, he helped her up and followed her into the parlor. Together they had watched the sun rise over the crystalline white world and afterward had indulged in hot cocoa and macaroons—a forbidden luxury to Annabelle at such an hour. But he'd put his finger to his lips and teasingly whispered, "Our secret."

The memory of that shared morning with Lawrence warmed her now, and she smiled. "I always have liked to greet the new day. I feel that if God goes to all the trouble to start each morning with beauty such as this, I should be grateful enough to see and enjoy it."

He nodded, looking to the east where the sky was now a mixture of muted violets, soft pinks, and pale yellows surrounding a rose-colored sun, hazily reflected in the rippling wake of the *Titanic*. "Though I think it hardly any trouble for one so powerful as He," he said slowly and softly, almost as though he were speaking to himself and had forgotten her presence.

"What is it the Scriptures say?" he continued. " 'Bless the Lord, O my soul. O Lord my God, thou art very great; thou art clothed with honour and majesty. Who coverest thyself with light as with a garment: who stretchest out the heavens like a curtain: Who layeth the beams of his chambers in the waters: who maketh the clouds his chariot: who walketh upon the wings of the wind: Who maketh his angels spirits; his ministers a flaming fire: Who laid the foundations of the earth, that it should not be removed for ever. Thou coveredst it with the deep as with a garment: the waters stood above the mountains. At thy rebuke they fled; at the voice of thy thunder they hasted away.' "

Lawrence's deep, melodic voice sent tingles down Annabelle's spine. Her eyes widened in fascination. "I don't remember reading that," she murmured. "How wonderfully poetic! And you know it so well! I must find and read those verses. By any chance, do you know where they are found?"

"I learned that Scripture when I was a lad under my tutor's instruction. If I remember correctly, that Scripture is found in the Psalms." Lawrence shook his head ruefully. "I forgot to tell my manservant to pack my Bible, so I can't look it up. I'll have to secure another when we reach America."

"I brought my Bible with me!"

Lawrence marveled at how her face seemed to light up from within and her eyes sparkled as though with inner fire. He cleared his throat before speaking. "Why, that's wonderful, Annabelle. Perhaps later, after breakfast, you can bring your Bible and we can meet here?"

"Yes, that would be lovely," she said, suddenly shy.

"I must go now," Lawrence said. "I made an appointment to play squash with Mr. Frederick Wright, the racquet attendant. Otherwise, I would stay."

Annabelle felt her cheeks go hot and she knew she was blushing. His words and the way he was looking at her caused her to feel a little breathless, renewing dreams for a romance between them. "Until this afternoon, then."

"I look forward to it, Annabelle." He tipped his hat to her with a smile, then turned to go. She watched him stride away, his carriage erect and certain, until he disappeared through the companionway and she could see him no longer.

❧

Though she was nervous, Annabelle managed to eat a breakfast of shirred eggs, grilled mutton, scones with marmalade jam, and fresh fruit. Lawrence was quiet, and Annabelle hoped he didn't regret his hasty invitation to her earlier this morning.

She was relieved to see that Charlotte and her brother weren't in attendance. It didn't really surprise her, though. They hardly seemed the type to be early risers. Of course, the *Titanic* offered other dining options, and Annabelle supposed they *could* have visited the à la carte restaurant. But she didn't think that was the case. Given Charlotte's extreme interest in Annabelle's father, Annabelle doubted the flashy woman would dine anywhere but where he was.

Annabelle's eyes cut to Lawrence. With a sinking heart she saw that his face had a grim look as he sliced his tomato omelet. She had looked forward to their getting together for hours now, and she worried that he no longer felt the same way. He had seemed quite anxious to spend time with her earlier; perhaps he was thinking of Frances and now regretted his impulsive act. But no, he still thought Annabelle a child. She was no threat to Frances.

Her father blotted his mouth with his napkin, then turned to her. "Well, I'm for the Turkish baths I've been hearing so much about. What will you do this morning, Annabelle dear?"

"I, uh. . ." She hesitated, caught off guard by his sudden question after thirty minutes of silence.

"Perhaps we could talk for a bit then," Edward said with a smile. "That is, if you can spare me a moment."

"Of course, Father," she hastily assured him.

Lawrence rose from his chair. "If you both will excuse me, then?" He looked directly at her. "I look forward to our Bible study, Annabelle. I'll meet you on the boat deck at twelve o'clock, if that's agreeable with you?"

Annabelle flushed, feeling her father's curious gaze light on her. "Yes, that would be lovely," she said, relieved. It was obvious Lawrence was still in favor of the idea.

"Bible study?" her father asked incredulously, after Lawrence had left the table.

Annabelle picked up her cut-crystal glass and drank the last bit of orange juice, allowing time for her cheeks to cool.

"Yes, Father. Lawrence has always shared my love of the Scriptures," she said, setting her glass down on the table. "This morning he recited a remarkable Psalm about our mighty God making the clouds His chariot and walking on the wings of the wind, among other things. He has promised to show it to me."

"I wasn't aware the two of you met earlier today."

Annabelle felt her cheeks flame again. Why? It had all been perfectly innocent. "I was on the boat deck, watching the sunrise, and he came from the gymnasium. We met and talked." She idly ran a finger along the rim of her glass, staring at it.

"Ahem, well. . ." He cleared his throat. "Let us go into the reception room for a little more privacy, so that we may talk without interruption."

Nodding, Annabelle followed her father into the adjoining room. However, it was crowded, many people partaking in an after-breakfast coffee. Obviously frustrated, he led her up the staircase to the next level, where they found two empty chairs not far from the stairway yet far enough from a few other couples to allow them a private conversation.

"Whatever is the matter, Father?"

Edward slowly rubbed his thumb and fingers over his jaw and mustache. He studied the curved staircase, the oil painting on the wall, the muted lighting. His gaze lowered to the white tiles, interspersed with decorative dark brown tiles, beneath his feet.

Part of his mind appreciated the luxurious surroundings, while another part struggled with how to proceed with what he wanted to say. Finally, his gaze came to rest on his daughter, who looked completely baffled by this time, and he cleared his throat. "Annabelle, it has come to my attention that you don't approve of Mademoiselle Fontaneau. I wish to know why."

Now it was Annabelle's turn to squirm. She bit her lip and studied her hands. "She reminds me of a black widow spider."

Edward's eyes widened. *"What?"*

"They lure their mates to their webs, and when they're done with them, they kill them."

Edward shook his head in exasperation. "Annabelle, really! You're a young woman now and should act like one. Such fanciful imaginings are more suited to the mind of a child."

Annabelle's mouth narrowed, but she didn't respond.

"Mademoiselle Fontaneau is an interesting dinner partner, nothing more. Like me, she is lonely and seeks companionship.

However, I've no desire to further the relationship."

Annabelle's ears perked up. "Really, Father?"

"Of course not." He reached out and awkwardly patted her hand. "It's been eight years since your mother died and left me, but on the slim chance I might be able to find someone as wonderful as Cynthia, don't you think I would seek your approval before taking the relationship to another level?"

Annabelle looked down at her lap, feeling suddenly foolish for having so little faith in her father or his judgment. "I'm sorry, Father. I know I've behaved abominably."

"I understand, my dear. If anything is bothering you in the future, I trust you will come to me with it."

She nodded. Edward hesitated, wondering if he should tell her about last night's losses in the card game with Monsieur Fontaneau. No; now was not the time. Besides, tonight he planned to win it all back, so there would be little reason to speak of his embarrassing folly.

❧

Once Annabelle reached her stateroom, she picked up her Bible and *The Pilgrim's Progress* from the table, left her cabin, and went up the stairs to the boat deck. She was much too excited to do nothing until twelve o'clock, so she headed for the sunny deck early to wait for Lawrence.

Annabelle had read only two pages from her book when a childish voice piped near her ear, "Hello."

Looking up, Annabelle saw Missy standing next to the deck chair and smiled. With a fluffy blue bow in her blond curls, the little girl looked absolutely adorable. She wore a white linen dress with a square sailor collar that was lined in dark blue rickrack. A blond-headed doll with a painted porcelain face was clutched tightly in her arms. Annabelle noted that the doll wore a dress similar to its owner's. She put down the book.

"Well, hello, Missy. How are you enjoying the excitement of being on a ship?"

The little girl shrugged. "It's okay, I s'pose. I've gone on one before when we went to Spain. This is Helena." She thrust the doll out for Annabelle's inspection.

"What a pretty doll. I see why you didn't want to lose her."

Maria walked up behind Missy. "Good morning, Miss Mooreland." Her tone was frosty and her dark gaze cool.

"Hello, Maria. Won't you call me Annabelle?"

Maria's eyes widened in an unguarded look of surprise, then narrowed perceptibly. "It is not—how do you say. . .proper—for me to do so. I am only a governess." Her tone was bitter.

"But that's not true! You're my cousin—daddy said so."

"Hush, little *niña,*" the exotic woman hastily inserted, avoiding Missy's puzzled gaze. "You mustn't speak so. Your mother, she would not like it."

Annabelle was clearly interested, almost to the point of being rude and boldly asking what the child was talking about. But a sense of propriety saved her at the last moment. "Please, sit down," she said, motioning to the empty deck chair beside her. She'd been saving it for Lawrence. The sunny deck was crowded today, and Annabelle was grateful she'd found a spot early.

"We must be going, but thank you," Maria said quickly.

Blue eyes wide, Missy pouted and looked up at her governess. "I asked Mama about strangers; she said once you meet someone, then she isn't a stranger anymore."

Maria exhaled, exasperated. "It's not that, Missy. Your mother made it clear that you were to have a nap this afternoon."

"But I don't want a nap!" the little girl insisted. "They're for babies. I'm going to be five tomorrow." She straightened proudly, looking up at Maria. "Besides, Helen Lorraine doesn't have to take naps!"

"Tomorrow's your birthday?" Annabelle asked softly, noting the rebellious pout of the rosy lips and the blazing blue eyes and trying to divert Missy to a happier topic.

Missy nodded. "And Mama is having a party for me in the res'raunt." Instantly she brightened. "Can Miss Annabelle come to my party, Maria? Please? I'll be good and take a nap."

Maria looked totally flustered. "Missy, I–I am certain Miss Mooreland has other plans."

Missy quickly turned to Annabelle. "Do you?"

Always honest, Annabelle admitted, "Well, no, not at the moment."

"See!" the little girl demanded of her nanny.

Annabelle felt bad to put Maria in such a position and quickly spoke up. "Missy, your mother and father don't know me. Perhaps they would prefer to have only the family celebrate."

Missy shook her blond head furiously. "Daddy's not on the boat with us—he's in Spain. And Mama already said she wants to meet you. Oh, please say you'll come!"

Annabelle looked helplessly to Maria, who looked resigned. "The party will be at the Café Parisian at 12:30 tomorrow afternoon," she stated indifferently. "If you want to come, I am certain *Doña* Ortega won't mind." She took Missy's hand. "Come, Missy. We have taken too much of Miss Mooreland's time."

"Bye, Miss Annabelle." The little girl looked over her shoulder as her nanny pulled her away. "I'll see you tomorrow!"

Annabelle watched and wondered. There was certainly a mystery there. She looked forward to going to the party tomorrow and meeting the as yet unseen *Doña* Ortega. So. . . Missy's father was a Spanish don. Strange that none of his dark looks showed in his golden-haired, blue-eyed daughter. And why wasn't he here? Missy had said he was in Spain. . . .

"Hello."

Startled, Annabelle turned and looked up into Lawrence's amused blue eyes. "Oh! Is it twelve o'clock already?"

He sat down in the empty deck chair beside her. "No, only eleven-thirty. I came early."

His soft-spoken words seemed deep with meaning, or maybe she just wanted them to sound that way. Feeling her cheeks warm, she looked down at her lap.

"I see you've brought your Bible," he said quickly. "If you'll allow me, I'll show you the Scripture passage I referred to this morning."

"Oh, yes! Please do," she said with a smile.

Lawrence took the black leather book and flipped through the thin pages. Annabelle watched, noting his strong hands and slender fingers. A gold signet ring bearing his family crest gleamed from his right hand. Her gaze lifted higher, to his face, and she studied him as he perused the pages.

He had taken off his hat when he sat down, and the ocean breeze moved through his thick dark hair, teasing the locks as they played over his smooth forehead. His eyelids beneath straight brows were lowered, shielding his remarkable eyes. His nose was straight, his jaw strong, his lips well shaped, sensitive. Not for the first time Annabelle wondered how it would feel to be kissed by them.

"Ah! Here it is—Psalm 104." He raised his head, fixing her with his warm gaze. Quickly she lowered her eyes to the page, flustered.

Lawrence wondered why her face turned red and why her hands shook when she took the book, but he didn't comment. Instead he intently studied her as she bent her head to read the passage.

She really had changed in four years' time. She still had the same pert nose he'd always thought so cute, and her lips were pink—a little fuller perhaps. A few dark, curly strands had come loose from her upswept bun, and for the first time he thought it a shame that fashion required women to wear their hair up. He remembered what a thick mane of it she had. Her face had lost all the baby fat and had thinned with maturity, bringing into relief her delicate cheekbones. The freckles were gone, but on closer inspection he was almost relieved to see a few light ones sprinkled over the bridge of her nose. A strange desire filled him to touch her cheek and see if it was really as soft as it looked—like satiny velvet. Her thickly lashed, emerald-colored eyes lifted to his face, and he swallowed—hard.

"Oh, but this is simply fascinating!" she exclaimed. "I never knew this was in here. The Psalms are quite beautiful."

"Annabelle," he said softly after a moment. "Please don't tell me you haven't been keeping up in reading the Word."

She lowered her eyes, a trifle sheepish. "Just the Old Testament. It's always been a bit difficult for me to understand—except when you explained the verses to me. You always had a wonderful way of making the Scriptures come alive, Lawrence. But when you didn't come home from university your last year, there was no one to talk to. And then we left Uncle William's house, and, well. . ." She shrugged and looked away.

But Lawrence understood and felt bad. During his last year at university, he'd gone with his roommate, Theodore, to his home during breaks. He supposed the least he could have done was write a cheery letter or two just to let Annabelle know someone cared. How lonely life must have been for her these past years!

He remembered the heavy atmosphere at Mooreland Hall, the constant animosity between the brothers—Annabelle's father and her uncle—and the huge, empty rooms devoid of children. . .except for one lonely little girl. Later his mother had told him that Annabelle and her father had moved to the empty caretaker's cottage on her uncle's property. And last year when he'd taken Frances to the annual spring soirée at Mooreland Hall, Annabelle hadn't been among the guests. He'd never forgotten her—their friendship had been too special for that. But once Lawrence had graduated, Frances had consumed most of his time.

He gave Annabelle's hand a gentle squeeze. "Well, I'm here now. So allow me to give you a brief lesson on the Psalms. They were mostly written by King David and deal with praising the Lord. However, there also are many Psalms that deal with crying out to the Lord in times of trouble. One thing the Psalms all have in common, though, is that they abound with poetry." He smiled. "If I remember correctly, you excelled in that area."

"Oh, yes! I loved it when we read from my book of sonnets together." Her eyes danced as she met his gaze. "But how I despised Latin! I'm quite sure I never would have understood it if you hadn't helped me, Lawrence."

"That's what friends are for," he said softly. "And I'll always be your friend."

Her face instantly clouded, and she looked down at her lap.

"Why the sad face all of a sudden, Annabelle?"

She shook her head.

"Annabelle? Don't you want to be my friend anymore?" he said in a mock-sad voice, trying to lighten the situation. He gently put his hand under her chin, forcing her to look up, and for one brief moment he was able to see what bloomed in her heart.

His eyes widened. "Annabelle. . .I. . ."

She rose before he could say more. "I have to go now," she murmured. But before she could hurry away, he grabbed her hand.

"Annabelle, listen to me—"

"Please, Lawrence—don't." She looked beyond him, refusing to meet his eyes, and noticed that several other passengers had curiously turned to look their way. "Let me go. We're drawing attention," she said quietly. Immediately he dropped her hand.

A group of rowdy boys raced by, laughing as they chased each other down the deck and abruptly stopping a few feet away when an officer blocked them and sternly reprimanded them. The incident was just what Annabelle needed to make her exit. Turning, she escaped to the nearby companionway and disappeared before Lawrence could rise and follow.

six

Annabelle took a small bite of her watercress sandwich, her mind a million miles away. She picked up her teacup and put it to her lips.

"And how's that nice young man o' yours?"

"Excuse me?" Annabelle almost choked on her tea and set it down quickly on its saucer, avoiding Maggie Brown's shrewd eyes.

"The man I saw you with on deck yesterday mornin'. A gentleman if ever I saw one. When I was goin' to the lounge, he gave a little bow as I stepped off the elevator and moved aside for me to pass. Made me feel like royalty, he did!"

Embarrassed, Annabelle looked away. Two young children sat on the floor nearby, playing a game.

"He's not my young man," Annabelle said softly, watching as the tots rolled a ball back and forth. "He's just a dear friend."

"Hmmm, a pity. He looks like a right fine catch," Maggie said, her sharp eyes lowering to Annabelle's slim fingers tightly gripping the handle of her teacup. "Well, never mind."

Annabelle picked up the silver teapot and managed to pour more into her cup without spilling it, though her hands were shaking. "Do you have any children, Mrs. Brown?"

"Oh, please, call me Maggie," the older woman said. " 'Mrs. Brown' sounds like you're talkin' to my husband's mother."

Annabelle allowed a small smile. "Maggie, then."

"Yes, a boy and a girl—Larry and Helen."

"And what does your husband do for a living. . ." Annabelle broke off and bit her lip, suddenly remembering what Maggie had told her the other day. "I'm sorry. I shouldn't have asked that."

Maggie chuckled and waved her hand, shooing away Annabelle's worries. "Now, honey, don't you fret. Ain't nothin' you can say to get me riled. You're much too sweet a child." Maggie reached for another sandwich. "James discovered gold quite a few years back—made a fortune off it. I'd say he probably uncovered enough gold to choke an elephant!"

"Really? How interesting," Annabelle said softly, now accustomed to Maggie's sledgehammer wit. She'd been in the woman's presence long enough to know Maggie Brown was in a class all her own, and Annabelle rather liked the older woman's colorful character. When she wasn't asking personal questions, that is.

They talked a bit longer, about family and friends, and Annabelle told Maggie what she remembered of Manhattan and her aunt who lived in New Jersey, making a mental note to check with her father and find out if he'd sent Aunt Christine a telegram informing her of their expected arrival time.

Unable to locate her father, Annabelle gave up and walked to her stateroom to study her Bible. She was looking forward to reading a few more of the Psalms. Upon entering, Annabelle found Sadie laying out her things for dinner.

"Sadie, you don't have to do that now," Annabelle said as she scanned the room for her leather-covered Bible, finally locating it on a chair by her bed. "Dinner is hours away."

Sadie blushed furiously, averting her gaze. "Well, actually, miss, I wanted to get everything ready now. I, um. . ." She wrung her hands. "I have plans for this evening. That is, if you won't be needing me," she hastily added.

Annabelle studied her flustered maid. "Not at all, Sadie. Feel free to take time for yourself. I'm relieved to see you up and around and feeling better. You deserve some private time."

"Thank you, Miss Annabelle," Sadie said, lowering her eyes.

Annabelle studied her critically. "Why, I think you look better than you have in months. You're positively glowing! This ocean air must be good for you."

Sadie flushed an even deeper red but didn't respond except

to say, "Yes, I feel fine now. I'll return at six to help you dress for dinner, Miss Annabelle. And thank you again."

Annabelle watched as Sadie hurried out, then turned to look at the silk dress hanging on the door. Cut simply, the gossamer ivory gown was trimmed with subtle threads of shiny silver, a silver satin underskirt shimmering beneath it. The filmy capelike sleeves were made of the same gauzy material as the dress and ended in a ruffle above the elbows. The gown, when it caught the glow of the electric torches, shimmered like trapped moonlight.

It was one of Annabelle's favorite dresses, making her feel like a princess whenever she wore it. She approved Sadie's choice and decided on the jewelry she would wear.

Afterward, she picked up her Bible and began reading. Poring over the poetic Psalms, she wondered about the men who wrote them, all the while being drawn closer to the One about whom they'd been written.

❧

During dinner, Annabelle noticed that Charlotte seemed rather high-strung, laughing a bit too strangely and doubling her efforts to attract the attention of Annabelle's father. As if that were a problem. However, Annabelle did notice a reserved air about her father tonight; he still smiled at Charlotte and paid a great deal of attention to her, but something in his manner toward her seemed to have changed.

Annabelle took a bite of her peaches in chartreuse jelly, chewing thoughtfully. Several meaningful looks passed between Monsieur Fontaneau and his sister, puzzling Annabelle. He seemed to be quietly demanding something, and Charlotte seemed. . .fearful? The woman suddenly let out a gay laugh, no sign of fear on her face, and Annabelle felt certain she must have been mistaken.

Lawrence's smooth, rich voice disrupted her musings. "You're rather quiet tonight."

Annabelle turned to face him, her eyes briefly fastening on his collar before looking beyond him. "Am I? I suppose I've nothing to say," she said, realizing she sounded a bit rude, but still embarrassed about their earlier encounter.

Lawrence wanted to bring up the afternoon's conversation, but with a feeling of frustration, he realized now was not the time. "Oh, you're wrong, Annabelle, you've always had plenty to say," he drawled, though not unkindly. She looked at him sharply, which was what he'd intended. At least now she wasn't avoiding him as she'd been doing all evening. "Tell me, have you read any more in the Psalms?" he asked, now that he had her full attention.

Annabelle bit her lip, then nodded, carefully setting her spoon on her plate. "Yes, I have. King David certainly was a poet, wasn't he? I know He was gifted with the harp and often sang beautiful songs to the Lord, like you once told me—and so many of the Psalms are filled with praise to the Creator." Her fine brows drew together in puzzlement. "Still, I was amazed to see how many Psalms deal with God delivering David from danger."

"You must remember, David often had to flee for his life from his enemy King Saul. David knew what real danger was, having come up against it countless times." She nodded, and he continued, "We could take a lesson from him in how to deal with danger, if the time ever comes for us to face it. Even in his most trying times, David never lost faith, always trusting the Lord would save him."

Annabelle idly picked up her spoon again, her expression thoughtful. "I find that amazing. I've never personally dealt with anything life-threatening. Not like my sister or my mother did." She looked up at him. "Have you ever experienced real danger, Lawrence?"

"I was thrown off a horse once when I was learning to ride," he admitted. "But besides cuts and scrapes and the few broken bones I acquired—as rambunctious boys often obtain while growing up—I've never faced any real danger."

"Were you really rambunctious?" Annabelle asked with a smile. "Somehow, I can't picture you that way. You've always been such a gentleman."

He leaned back, relieved that she was herself again. "Oh, yes, I was quite a little scamp. But I suppose most young boys go through that stage." He studied her, a mischievous light dancing in his eyes. "And I remember what a little hoyden you were, always tearing your new pinafores, climbing fences and trees, riding the horses with total abandon. I don't envy your maid her job. You always were such a spirited thing," he teased. But she wasn't one bit amused.

"Lawrence, must you always see me the way I was years ago? Take a good look. I've changed, in case you haven't noticed. I'm a young woman now—I enjoy teas and crumpets and balls. I prefer Paris fashions and Elizabeth Barrett Browning sonnets to pinafores and Mother Goose nursery rhymes. I was even engaged up until two weeks ago. . . ."

Shocked that she'd revealed such a thing and in such a way, Annabelle hurriedly looked down at her plate. She hadn't meant to tell Lawrence about Roger. But her words had come so fast and furiously—she was so frustrated with his constant little-girl comparisons—that it just slipped out.

There was a long pause before he spoke. "Annabelle, I apologize. Please understand that the image of you I had in my mind up until a few days ago was that of a little girl just on the verge of womanhood, and it may take some time for me to fully accept the changes. I can certainly see you're a young lady now, and I didn't mean any disrespect." She lifted her head and noticed how uncomfortable he looked. "I hadn't realized you were engaged," he added. "Do I know him?"

She shook her head. "I don't think so. His name is Roger—Roger Fieldhall. I met him at a party at my uncle's house."

"The polo player?" At her nod, he asked, "What happened?"

She grimaced. "I became aware he wouldn't be the type to keep his wedding vows once we married. It's no longer important," she said, not wanting to discuss Roger with him. "I'm just relieved I discovered the truth in time."

"Did he hurt you?"

Annabelle felt warmth flow through her at the almost angry, protective tone of Lawrence's voice—evidence he must still care about her a little. She looked back down at her dessert plate. "No, he didn't hurt me—not really. It was more a case of wounded pride and embarrassment. I never loved him and even told him so, but he seemed to think I'd fall for him in time. I'm ashamed to say his offer of a partnership in the glittering world of his stardom is what caused me to accept his proposal in the first place." *That and the fact I knew your love was for another, Lawrence,* she added silently.

Her eyes nervously flicked upward; she feared she'd see his expression filled with disdain for the fickle creature he probably now thought her to be. Her heart fluttered at the soft look he gave her. "I'm sorry you had to go through something like that, Annabelle. I know firsthand what a rotten experience it can be."

His words alerted her. "What do you mean?"

He looked around the dining room and watched as several guests departed for the adjoining room before answering her. "It appears dinner is over. Would you care to join me in the reception room? We can continue our conversation there."

She nodded and turned to tell her father, realizing with shock that at some point he'd torn his attention away from Charlotte and had been observing her and Lawrence. Annabelle's face grew hot. How long had he been listening?

"An excellent idea, Lord Caldwell. I'd like to visit the reception room myself and listen to the musicians play," he said, his eyes twinkling first at Lawrence and then at Annabelle. "Yesterday, when they played near the grand stairway, I was in rather a hurry to reach my stateroom and didn't pay much attention. And during dinner they play so softly, it's a bit difficult to hear them. I can scarcely hear them now."

Annabelle looked at him, shock written in her eyes. Except for the day they'd boarded, her father usually went to the smoking room for brandy and cigars after dinner. Why was he acting so out of character? Unless. . .unless he thought she needed a chaperone because Lawrence was romantically interested in her. *Oh Father, if only you knew.*

And yet, what had Lawrence meant by his cryptic remark earlier?

seven

Annabelle moved with the others to the spacious reception room, barely aware of the group of talented musicians playing a gay tune. At the moment, all she was aware of was Lawrence by her side, his hand above her elbow where the long glove ended, as he guided her to a small table next to a tall plant with long, slender green fronds. Her father walked behind them, Charlotte clinging to his arm like a love-starved octopus, and Eric beside her.

Lawrence took the seat next to Annabelle. "They are rather accomplished, aren't they?" he asked after a few minutes had passed and the orchestra had moved into another song.

"Yes," Annabelle said a bit impatiently, wishing he would continue their earlier conversation.

After a few awkward minutes had passed, her father abruptly spoke up. "There's Colonel Gracie—quite an interesting fellow. Wrote a book on Chickamauga—one of the battles of the Civil War in America," he added for the women's benefit. "I need to discuss an important matter with him. If you'll excuse me for a moment?" He nodded to the others, then rose from his chair.

Annabelle looked across the room to the dignified gentleman with the bushy dark mustache. Colonel Gracie seemed to be deeply engaged in conversation with Mr. Straus. Did father really have business with the colonel, or was he merely trying to find a polite way to escape Charlotte's clutches?

Eric whispered something to Charlotte and they excused themselves, moving to the doorway. Annabelle turned to Lawrence. "Please tell me what you meant earlier when you said you knew firsthand how terrible an experience such as

I went through with Roger could be," she asked, a little breathlessly.

Lawrence sighed. "Do you remember Frances Davenport? Her father's estate adjoins Fairview."

Remember? How could she ever forget? She nodded dismally. "I'd heard you two were engaged."

His eyes widened in shock. "Who told you that?"

Annabelle looked down, embarrassed. She didn't want to tell him she'd overheard one of the servants at Mooreland Hall gossiping with another a few months before Annabelle moved with her father to the cottage. The handsome viscount's activities had often been secretly discussed among the people of Fairhaven, though Annabelle never took part in such talk.

When she didn't answer, Lawrence said, "It's true my parents wanted us to marry, but Frances and I were never engaged."

Annabelle quickly lifted her head and saw the sincerity in his eyes. "You were never engaged?" Her heart stopped, then began to race, keeping time with the tune "Glowworm," which the musicians were now enthusiastically playing.

"No." He leaned back in his chair, his eyes going to the few dancing couples on the floor. "I never felt comfortable around Frances, though for my parents' sake, I did try to make a go of it with her. But she wasn't the lady everyone thought her to be." He looked toward Annabelle then. "A few months ago I discovered she was secretly having an affair with a married man. She only wanted a union between us because she was Davenport's stepdaughter and wasn't entitled to the large inheritance her stepbrothers were. She was attracted to the Caldwell fortune."

"Oh, Lawrence, I'm so sorry," Annabelle murmured, vividly remembering the haughty blond she'd seen dancing with Lawrence at the Christmas ball five years ago. His news about Frances didn't surprise her; but his news that he wasn't engaged did.

"Don't be, Annabelle. I'm not wearing my heart on my sleeve, I assure you. I never loved Frances and am grateful I found out her true character before it was too late."

Her mind a whirlwind of conflicting thoughts, Annabelle nodded as if in a daze. All these years she'd thought Lawrence loved Frances, that they were engaged and would one day marry. For so long she'd yearned for Lawrence to look at her with eyes of love but had thought it hopeless and had avoided his company, resigning herself to the idea of a loveless marriage with Roger. Up until a few months ago, she and Lawrence had been promised to others. . .but now they were both free.

"Annabelle, are you well?" he asked, his voice laced with concern. "You look a little strange."

She blinked and smiled at him. "Oh, yes. I'm wonderful."

He looked at her oddly, obviously puzzled by her sudden giddiness and the dreamy way she'd spoken, but he only gave her one of his boyish grins. "Something just occurred to me, Miss Mooreland," he said formally. "In all the years we've been acquainted, we've never danced with one another. Would you care to join me in a waltz?"

Her smile grew wider. "I shall be more than happy to, Lord Caldwell," she answered, just as formally. Her head was in the clouds as she took his arm and walked with him across the tiled floor.

Lawrence took her right hand in a warm clasp, at the same time lightly placing his other hand against her waist; then they began gracefully moving to the music of the stringed instruments. Annabelle followed his lead, though in her nervousness, her feet fumbled twice. She could feel the heat of his hand through the material of her dress and had to remind herself to breathe.

Dancing with him was as wonderful as Annabelle had always imagined it would be. The look in his eyes nearly melted her, and she felt her cheeks grow hot while her head slowly started to spin. They moved so well together; Annabelle was sorry when the Strauss waltz ended and the musicians went into a ragtime tune. But he didn't let her go. A few other couples twirled around them while they stood motionless in the middle of the floor and stared at one another.

"Oh, Lawrence, I love you," Annabelle breathed.

Her mouth dropped open in shock when she realized she'd spoken her thoughts aloud. Startled, he stared at her, his eyes growing as wide as hers now were, and she hurriedly broke away from him, almost tripping on her gown in her haste.

"I–I mean I love being with you. . .in your company," she blurted out, her face bright red. "I enjoy the friendship we share." She bit her lower lip. "I'm suddenly feeling quite weary. I think I'll turn in now. Good night."

He shook his head. "I can't let you walk unescorted this late at night, Annabelle," he said, his voice soft.

"Oh, no, please," she put in hastily, inching backward. "I know my way about, and there are many stewards and stewardesses throughout the ship—that is, if I should need assistance of any kind, which I'm certain I won't. But thank you for offering, Lawrence," she said quickly, her words falling over one another in her haste to depart. She almost tripped on the hem of her gown again as she took another quick step backward. "I'll see you at breakfast in the morning."

Turning, she escaped across the wide floor and up the grand staircase, like a startled doe in flight.

Stunned, Lawrence watched her rapid ascent. Had she really meant what she'd first said. . .that she loved him? He remembered the other day on the boat deck when she'd run away. For a moment he'd thought he'd seen something in her eyes when she briefly looked at him. Later, he was certain he'd been mistaken; yet her behavior afterward had been rather strange. . .as it was now.

He had practically convinced himself they could be nothing more than friends, certain Annabelle would be uncomfortable with the six-year difference in their ages. But what if he were wrong?

Lawrence made a hasty inspection of the room, searching for Edward to tell him Annabelle had left, so he wouldn't worry if he couldn't find her later. However, Edward was nowhere in sight.

Striding across the wide floor and up the grand staircase, Lawrence hurried after Annabelle, uncomfortable at the thought of her roaming the huge ship alone.

❧

Annabelle's heels clicked a sharp staccato across the smooth, polished floor as she hurried in the direction of her stateroom. She couldn't believe she'd actually blurted out to Lawrence that she loved him! She had thought it so often, and the shock of realizing he wasn't engaged to Frances coupled with the wonderful feeling of being in his arms must have loosened her tongue. Oh, how could she ever face him again?

He already thought her immature; now he probably thought she had a silly schoolgirl crush on him after the way she'd acted. But it was so much more than that! How could she avoid him these next few days? Unless, of course, she stayed in her room and starved. . . . She wondered if the ship offered room service. Surely a ship as luxurious as this would.

Her mouth turned grim. *You're acting just like the child he thinks you to be, Annabelle Mooreland. Stop being so dramatic! There is a little less than a week of this voyage left, and then you'll probably never see him again.*

Ignoring the pain this thought produced, she stopped walking, suddenly remembering she'd not spoken with her father about the matter of contacting her aunt. Should she discuss it with him in the morning? But what if it slipped her mind again? It wouldn't do for them to arrive unexpectedly. Yet she just couldn't go back down there and face Lawrence right now!

She bit her lip and peered down the carpeted corridor that led to her room, then she looked toward the elevators. To her surprise, Charlotte stepped off one of the lifts, alone, and hurried away, not noticing Annabelle. Which most likely meant that Annabelle's father had gone to the first-class smoke room.

But that presented yet another problem. Women weren't allowed inside the gentlemen's private sanctuary, where the men often retired after dinner to smoke cigars and drink brandy. Yet she had to talk to him. Annabelle took the elevator to A-deck, approached the door to the smoke room, and stopped, having second thoughts now that she was here. She supposed she could send a steward to fetch her father, but would he consider her errand frivolous and become irritated with her for interrupting him?

Well, it's too late to back down now, Annabelle thought determinedly as she looked at the door to the wealthy gentlemen's inner sanctum. Glancing around, she was dismayed to see none of the stewards who usually were in abundance wherever one looked. Frustrated, she walked around the upper balcony to the corridor, relieved to spot a white-coated steward coming from one of the rooms, an empty tray in his hand.

"Excuse me?" Annabelle queried, motioning to him.

Immediately he walked down the aisle. "Yes, miss?"

Annabelle paused, a bit embarrassed. "I was wondering if you could deliver a message to one of the gentlemen in the smoke room—a Mr. Mooreland—and tell him that his daughter desires to speak with him right away?"

"Of course, miss." He gave a slight bow and quickly walked into the smoke room. Soon Edward Mooreland's silver head came through the door, and Annabelle hurried up to him.

"Annabelle! What's this all about? Couldn't it have waited 'til morning?"

She blinked and bit the inside of her lip. She should have waited. Oh, why hadn't she waited?

Running his fingers over the lower part of his face, he gruffly cleared his throat. "I'm sorry if I was abrupt," he said, his voice now controlled. "Now tell me, what's the problem?" He took her elbow, steering her away from the door.

Annabelle relaxed, though her father still seemed a trifle uneasy. Perhaps he was just tired. "I wanted to know if you'd contacted Aunt Christine," she explained hurriedly, now feeling her mission wasn't as important as she had first thought and wanting to be done with it. "The rooms of the house will need airing, and the servants need to be notified of our arrival."

His face took on a strange expression. "The house. . .of course. . .the house," he said under his breath as though he were speaking to himself and had forgotten her existence. He blinked and shook his head. "I'd forgotten that little detail. Don't concern yourself, Annabelle. I'll send a wire tomorrow."

"Very well, Father," Annabelle said quickly, taking a few steps backward. "I'll see you at breakfast, then. Good night."

Edward gave a vague nod. His mind was so involved in the interrupted card game, he was unaware that Annabelle had hurried away unescorted. Abruptly he turned and entered the room, striding across the patterned carpet to his table. With barely concealed irritation, he noted Monsieur Fontaneau was no longer there.

Upon his return, a gentleman at another table turned and, after taking a puff off his cigar, nodded to the other empty seat. "Monsieur Fontaneau also had urgent business that warranted his leaving. He said to tell you that he would try to finish with it as quickly as possible."

Resigned, Edward nodded, sat down, and lit his pipe.

❧

Annabelle hurried down the stairs, relieved when she had reached B-deck. However, she'd taken the staircase closest to the stern, rather than the one she usually took near the bow of the ship where her room was located. So she still had a long walk ahead of her.

The corridors remained empty, and Annabelle felt completely isolated, her senses heightened by the eerie stillness of the long, carpeted hallway. Most of the other passengers were in the restaurants, reception areas, lounges, or on the promenades, and many had already retired for the night beyond these very doors. But that fact didn't make Annabelle feel much better.

"The Lord is my light and my salvation," she breathed,

"whom shall I fear? the Lord is the strength of my life; of whom shall I be afraid?" It was all she could remember of the Twenty-seventh Psalm that she'd read earlier that morning, but it helped to ease the tension a little. However, when Annabelle reached the grand staircase, her uneasiness returned and multiplied. Monsieur Fontaneau walked down the stairs, heading in her direction.

"Good evening, Mademoiselle Mooreland," he said smoothly, his eyes roaming over her, making her shiver. "You shouldn't walk unescorted zis late at night. You never know what manner of man may be lurking on ze ship."

Annabelle's blood turned to ice in her veins. "If you'll excuse me, Monsieur Fontaneau, I must be going to my room now."

Unmoving, he stood in front of her, blocking her way to the corridor that led to her room. She swallowed and looked up into his dark blue eyes, her heart hammering at the bold look in them.

"You have left ze dance early. Such a lovely woman as you should not confine herself to her room so much of ze time."

Her throat went dry at his silky words. He lifted a hand to her cheek, brushing it with the back of his knuckles, making her shiver again. Then his hand dropped to the diamond pendant around her neck, lifting it with his fingertips. "Your beauty rivals even zese exquisite jewels you wear and zose shining from your hair."

Annabelle took a step backward, her hand nervously fluttering to her tiara. She said the first thing that came to mind. "They were my mother's. They've been in the family for generations."

"Ah. . .rare jewels for rare beauty. Zey are privileged to be in ze company of one such as zeir mistress."

Annabelle swallowed, her eyes darting around the empty room. "Excûse me, Monsieur Fontaneau, but I really must bid you good night."

She stepped around him, but his strong hands flew upward

and firmly took hold of her upper arms. Her head snapped up, and she stared at him in shock. His face loomed closer; his eyes were electrifying, dangerous. . . .

"Annabelle?"

At the sound of Lawrence's brusque voice, her would-be attacker let his hands drop from her arms and took a step back, his head lifting to look behind her. Annabelle exhaled a shaky breath, and turning, she hurried to her rescuer, clutching his upper arm in panic. "Lawrence," she breathed in relief, forgetting her former humiliation with him.

His brow drew down into a frown as he looked at her, then at the Frenchman. Annabelle studied Lawrence's rigid, unsmiling features. She glanced Eric's way, then turned back to Lawrence. The look of challenge passing between the two men was obvious; she knew conflict could ignite and flash out of control in a moment—unless she stopped it.

"Is there a problem, Annabelle?" Lawrence asked softly, dangerously, never breaking eye contact with Eric. "Was this *gentleman* bothering you?" He said the word sarcastically.

"No, no. I'm all right—really," she quickly assured him. "Monsieur Fontaneau was merely warning me of the hazards of walking unescorted this late at night. I suppose I became rather anxious, which explains my unusual behavior."

Lawrence broke his stare with Eric to study her face. "Are you certain?" His voice was steel wrapped in velvet.

"Oh, yes. It was of no matter, Lawrence, I assure you."

Eric spoke for the first time. "I will take your leave now, Mademoiselle Mooreland. Remember to be more careful in ze future." He nodded to both of them. "*Bonsoir.*"

Lawrence watched Eric make his way up the staircase, and Annabelle clearly saw a nervous tic in Lawrence's jaw. Realizing she still tightly grasped his arm, she dropped her hands and took a step away. "I should go now. It's been a rather long day."

Without a word, he took her elbow and walked with her down the carpeted corridor to her room. She silently admitted she was grateful for his protection; her heart still pattered madly against her rib cage from the narrow escape. Or was it his close proximity that caused her heart to race?

At the door to her stateroom, they stopped. Annabelle felt her cheeks grow hot. Suddenly feeling a bit awkward, she looked down. "Thank you, Lawrence."

"It was my pleasure, Annabelle. I hope you have pleasant dreams." His low, soothing voice brought her head up. Flustered, she watched as he took her gloved hand in his and slowly raised it to his lips, his ice-blue eyes never leaving hers. "Good night."

"Good night," she said on a shaky breath. Turning quickly, she slipped into her stateroom, shut the door behind her, and leaned against the smooth wood. Taking a few deep breaths, she told herself that his unexpected gesture had been nothing more than the customary act of a gentleman escorting a lady to her room and bidding her good night. Still, she hoped it was much more than that. . . .

eight

"Miss Annabelle? Ma'am?"

Annabelle groggily pulled the covers closer around her ears, trying to drown out the insistent voice. "Go 'way."

"But Miss Annabelle. It's ten o'clock in the morning. . . ."

Sadie's words were like a dousing of ice cold water. Annabelle's eyes flew open and she quickly sat up. "Ten o'clock, you say? Oh, how could I have slept so late," she moaned, throwing off the covers and hastening out of bed.

Sadie quickly gathered Annabelle's things together and helped her dress. "I'm sorry, miss. I suppose it's my fault—you missing breakfast and all. I–I didn't get to my room 'til late last night and didn't wake up 'til fifteen minutes ago."

Pulling on heavy stockings, Annabelle shook her head. "No, it's not your fault. I didn't retire until quite late myself."

She'd lain in bed last night, unable to sleep, her mind a hodgepodge of thoughts. She'd relived the frightening encounter with Monsieur Fontaneau but also the dance and the wonderful feeling of being in Lawrence's arms while they waltzed, and later, the look in his eyes when he'd kissed her hand. Had it been her imagination, or did he, too, desire more than friendship?

After Sadie helped her with her corset, Annabelle slipped a lilac dress with a white lace inset and long lace sleeves over her head, and Sadie fastened the pearl buttons running along the back. Suddenly Annabelle stiffened as she remembered something.

"Sadie, I'm in rather a dilemma. It seems I've been invited to a party—a child's birthday—and I've no gift to bring."

Sadie's brow furrowed. "A child's birthday, you say? Hmmm. I know of nothing. . ." Her voice trailed away, then her eyes suddenly brightened. "Wait a minute! I met the most delightful young woman on the second-class promenade. She crochets and knits all sorts of things. She told me she has a few items she's finished and hopes to find a place to sell them in America. Maybe she'd sell some of her work to you."

Annabelle's eyes gleamed as another thought came to her. "Oh, please find out, Sadie! The party is only a few hours away. See if she has a blanket—such as a baby would use."

"A baby?"

Annabelle laughed at her maid's stunned expression as she stopped in midflight. "Yes, a baby! Go on, I can fix my hair."

Humming to herself, Annabelle braided her dark tresses and wrapped the silky rope around her head, pinning it in place, then added a wide-brimmed hat loaded with lilac and cream blossoms.

Knowing she'd missed breakfast in the dining room, she ate in the expensive a la carte restaurant, which catered to special tastes. It was quite lovely with its deep pile rose carpeting, floral tapestry chairs, and light walnut furniture and paneling.

Annabelle wondered why her father hadn't come to her door to escort her to breakfast as he usually did. Remembering his abrupt behavior last night, she reasoned he might be ill this morning. Perhaps he had one of those nasty headaches that sometimes plagued him. She should check on him.

After a light gourmet meal, Annabelle hurried to her father's stateroom. She knocked on the door and waited, but he didn't answer. Mildly puzzled, she turned away, assuming he must have retired to what had become his favorite room—the men's smoking lounge. With a resigned sigh, she went to her room and retrieved her Bible, then climbed the stairs to the boat deck. She was sorry to have missed yet another sunrise and promised herself she wouldn't sleep late again while on this voyage.

A blast of cold air attacked her as she opened the door of the companionway. She pulled her jacket closer around her and easily found a chair. The boat deck wasn't crowded this morning, and few people strolled along the deck.

Annabelle shivered and opened her Bible to the Psalms. But the teasing wind snatched the page from her fingers and caused the rest of them to flutter madly. Sighing, she closed the leather cover, giving up. She looked out over the barely rippling ocean, half hoping Lawrence would come. But after ten minutes passed with no sign of him, Annabelle decided to seek warmth and went below.

❧

"Oh, Sadie! It's lovely," Annabelle murmured, holding up a snow-white blanket with tassels bordering its edges. Delicate pink flowers had also been embroidered along the edge. "And you even brought something to wrap it in—how clever of you!"

Sadie blushed as she handed Annabelle the brown paper and string. "A–a friend of mine is a steward on the ship, and he gave me this when I told him about the situation."

"How thoughtful of him. Please thank him for me."

Blushing, Sadie looked away and nodded. Idly wondering why her maid was acting so strangely, Annabelle shrugged it off, knowing she would need to leave soon for the party. She grabbed her reticule from the table and took out a couple of pound notes. "Give this to the woman and tell her for me that I think her workmanship is extraordinary. Get her name and where she will be staying; I may be in touch with her after we reach America."

Sadie took the generous amount of money and stuffed it in her bodice. "Her name is Myra Flannigan. I'll ask for her address." She bit her lip. "If you won't be needing me. . ."

Annabelle nodded. "Go and enjoy yourself. All too soon this voyage will be over, and you'll want as many memories as possible to share with your grandchildren someday."

As Sadie hurried away with a word of thanks, Annabelle wrapped the blanket, hoping Missy would like the small gift.

❧

Upon entering the Café Parisian, Annabelle felt as if she

were seeing it for the first time. She'd eaten here the day they'd left Southampton, but she'd been upset then.

The lights were dim, the carpeting a dark brick red. Carved white walls and ceiling matched the wicker furniture. Ivy-covered trellises along the walls provided a splash of refreshing color. Several young couples sat at the tables, eating delicate sandwiches and sipping coffee and aperitifs while listening to the low strains of music coming from the band in the adjoining reception room.

Annabelle easily spotted Missy, who looked adorable in a dark-blue velvet dress and crocheted white-lace collar. An image of what Missy would look like in twenty years sat beside the little girl, talking to her. Maria stood on the other side of Missy, picking up bits of discarded paper. Several other children sat around the small table and at the table next to it.

One of the children, a girl no more than four years old, shyly walked up to Annabelle. A huge ruffled bow sat atop the girl's dark hair, and she studied Annabelle with curious eyes, a finger in her mouth. Annabelle smiled, receiving a shy smile in return.

"Lorraine, dear, come here," a dark-headed woman sitting nearby said softly. The child turned and ran to the woman, but instantly turned her head, looking back at Annabelle.

"Miss Annabelle!" Missy exclaimed happily, receiving an instant rebuke from her mother to hold her voice down.

Annabelle took the remaining steps to the table and handed her package to Missy. "I'm sorry I'm late, Missy." She turned to the blond, who curiously looked at her, obviously wondering at the appearance of a stranger at her daughter's birthday party. "I'm Annabelle Mooreland," she said with a smile.

Doña Ortega nodded regally. "Missy has talked a great deal about you. It was kind of you to come." The words were gracious, but the woman's Dresden-blue eyes were cool, as was the expression on her smooth, china-doll face.

Annabelle's gaze shifted to the exotic woman standing

behind Missy. "Hello, Maria."

"Miss Mooreland," Maria said with a deferential nod.

An excited squeal erupted from Missy's mouth, earning another stern reprimand from her mother.

"Oh, Miss Annabelle," Missy gushed, blue eyes sparkling. "Now my Annabelle will have something to keep her warm!"

Annabelle raised her eyebrows, puzzled at the child's words, then smiled as Missy lifted a new, elegantly dressed doll with long, dark ringlets of hair for Annabelle's inspection.

"What a lovely doll," Annabelle said, relieved Missy had known for what purpose Annabelle had intended the gift.

As she watched Missy lovingly wrap the fuzzy material around her new doll, Annabelle felt grateful to the mystery woman who'd made such a fine present. She tried to recall the name Sadie had given her. Meg? No, not Meg. . .Myra. Yes that was it, Myra Flannigan. She fully intended to get in contact with the woman upon reaching America. Maybe Annabelle could help her set up her own business. Such craftsmanship shouldn't go unnoticed.

A smiling stewardess served red punch and thin slices of iced cake to the small party. Annabelle took a small bite of the rich cake, idly wondering at the strange relationship between Missy's mother and Maria. Not once since Annabelle arrived had Doña Ortega addressed Maria, except for a few curt orders. For the most part, both women ignored each other, and Annabelle could sense the dislike simmering between them.

Though Missy's mother was stunningly beautiful in her powder-blue, gauzy gown, there was a frosty look in her eyes and a downward tilt to her delicate mouth that warned of a cold nature. After several futile attempts at conversation with Doña Ortega, Annabelle wished Missy a happy birthday and left, grateful to escape the heavy atmosphere in the room.

❧

Annabelle tried to focus on the printed page, but her mind refused to concentrate. Where could her father be? She hadn't seen him all day—neither had anyone else she had asked.

She had hesitantly introduced herself to Colonel Gracie, upon seeing him leave the first-class lounge; he'd been sympathetic and had offered to go and look for her missing father. Annabelle hastily assured him that wasn't necessary, the memory of her father's angry behavior the night before coming to mind.

Not knowing what else to do, Annabelle then went to her room to retrieve *The Pilgrim's Progress,* deciding to visit the lounge and finish the last few chapters of the book. She'd easily found an empty chair and sat down, opening her book.

But as she sat there now—her eyes had skimmed over a paragraph three times and yet she still didn't know what she had read—she realized that trying to concentrate was futile. Sighing, she lifted her head to gaze out the curtained windows and studied the calm ocean.

"Hello, Annabelle."

Her heart jumped to her throat upon hearing the deep voice she loved so much. Willing her pulse rate to return to normal, she turned and looked up into Lawrence's serious gaze.

"May I join you?" he asked. Annabelle nodded, and Lawrence pulled a chair back from the table and sat down. "I was concerned when I didn't see you or your father at breakfast," he said as his eyes studied her, questioning.

A dread Annabelle couldn't name rose within her. "Father wasn't at breakfast?"

"Why, no. Didn't he eat with you? I'd assumed when I didn't see either of you that you'd both dined elsewhere."

She clenched her hands together in her lap and looked down. "Actually, I haven't seen him yet today."

Lawrence obviously sensed her distress, for his voice became soothing. "I'm certain there's no cause for alarm, Annabelle. Likely as not he's in the smoking lounge, or perhaps he went to visit the Turkish baths again. I wouldn't concern myself."

"Yes–yes, you're right. There's probably a simple explanation." But she knew she didn't sound very convincing.

"Would you like me to go look for him?"

Annabelle bit the inside of her lip, then raised her eyes to his. They were concerned and sympathetic, causing a warm glow to radiate inside her, chasing the gloom away. She smiled. "No. I'm probably overreacting. It's likely as you said, Lawrence—he simply made other plans without telling me first. His behavior was rather unusual last night."

He gave her an encouraging smile, for which she was grateful. There was a moment of companionable silence before he spoke. "I see you're continuing your studies on the pilgrimage of Christian." He nodded to the book on the table.

"Yes," she said with a small sigh. "Only today I can't seem to concentrate on the words. I'm afraid I can't get Christian through the Enchanted Garden. Every time I try, I lose concentration, and I fear he's doomed to stay there forever."

He grinned. "Perhaps what you need is a good dose of fresh air. Would you care to take a walk with me around the deck?"

"Oh, but it's so cold." She bit her lip, uncertain. "I suppose I could get my coat from my room, though. . . ." She really *did* want to walk with Lawrence.

He stood and held out his hand. "Shall we, then?"

"All right," Annabelle said a little shyly, still uncertain how things stood between them. Were they just friends or had their relationship entered another level? Oh, how she hoped it was the latter!

Before going to her room, Annabelle tried knocking on her father's door again. When she received no reply, she gave Lawrence a little shrug, acting as if she wasn't concerned. But she was. Somehow, she knew something was terribly wrong.

❧

Edward heard the insistent knocking attacking his brain and came out of his alcohol-induced sleep, groaning. He sat up and swung his legs over the side of the bed, wishing the terrible throbbing pain would stop. He didn't remember drinking *that* much.

The events of the previous night played themselves over in his fuzzy brain like some form of sadistic torture, and he dropped his head into his hands in agony. "Oh, Cynthia! What have I done? *What have I done!*" Rasping sobs shook his body as heavy chains of guilt wrapped around him, squeezing ruthlessly.

In one wild, reckless moment, he had succeeded in destroying his young daughter's future.

nine

"Ooh! It is rather cold, isn't it?" Annabelle gasped, pulling her fur coat closer around her.

"Would you prefer to go below?"

She looked sideways at Lawrence and saw a hint of disappointment in his eyes. "No, I'll be fine. I do enjoy the outdoors," she said with a smile.

"I know. It's something we've always had in common," Lawrence answered so softly, she almost didn't hear him.

They walked in companionable silence for a few moments, looking at the still ocean over the white balustrade.

"Isn't it unusual that the sea is so calm?" Annabelle asked, more to start a conversation than for any real desire to know. In the silence, terrible thoughts concerning the whereabouts of her father had clamored through her head, and she didn't want to give them free rein. "After my first voyage, and after hearing you read *Moby Dick* years ago, I was expecting at least one small storm."

Lawrence seemed thoughtful, then nodded. "Yes, I overheard several gentlemen—obviously well-seasoned travelers—talking yesterday. They, too, were commenting on the strange phenomenon. However, I think it rather a blessing, don't you?"

"Yes. It is a relief not to be tossed to and fro."

He smiled at her. "I agree. But I was referring to the fact that the captain has made remarkable time. We covered more miles yesterday than on Thursday, and, from what I understand, we will probably exceed yesterday's distance today. Because the waters are so calm, the ship is able to travel across the ocean much faster," he explained. "Therefore, it's a strong possibility we'll reach the shores of America sooner than planned."

His words brought a stab of pain to Annabelle's heart. Soon they would arrive in New York Harbor. And what then? Would she have to part ways with Lawrence? Would he just tip his hat and say good-bye? *Please, God. Don't let me lose him again.*

"Why so melancholy all of a sudden, Annabelle?" He stopped walking and turned to her. She stopped also.

Swallowing the tears threatening to choke her, she managed a small smile. "Was I? I suppose I was wondering what your plans were once we reach America. I was quite surprised to discover you aboard the *Titanic*. I mean, I couldn't possibly think what business a Caldwell would have in the States."

"Not business. . .pleasure. I've always had the wanderlust in my heart—the desire for adventure. Father realized it and encouraged me to take this voyage and visit friends who live in Manhattan. He hopes this bit of excitement will satisfy the adventuring spirit in me so that I can soon return to England and resume my duties as heir apparent," he said, with a boyish grin.

Remembering the stories Lawrence read to her before he went to university—of courageous knights embarking on dangerous quests, often rescuing damsels in distress, and ruthless pirates fighting daring captains on the high seas—Annabelle doubted the earl's plan would work concerning his son. Even now she could remember the gleam in Lawrence's eyes while he read to her.

"My mother's home is in Manhattan, also," she said softly. "That's where Father and I are going."

"Really. . . ," Lawrence said, seeming to consider something. "Would you mind if I called on you at your home in America?"

She held her breath, hardly daring to believe she'd heard him correctly. "As a friend?" she murmured.

He nodded, taking the wind out of her sails. But his next words buoyed her spirits again. "We will always be friends, Annabelle. But I was hoping to call on you as a suitor. That is, if the age difference between us doesn't concern you," he added quickly.

"Age difference?"

"The fact that we're six years apart."

Her look turned incredulous. "You're hardly an old man, Lawrence! Why, Father was eleven years older than Mama," she added, obviously surprising him, judging from his shocked expression. She nodded as if to emphasize her point. "He was thirty-five and she was twenty-four when they married. And they loved each other dearly.

"Oh, I'm certain they fought at times, but I've no recollection of them doing so. I do remember Mama telling me about a conflict between them a few days after I was born, though. You see, Father wanted to name me for my grandmother—his mother—but Mama insisted on naming me after her mother and sister, and for a while, Mama and Papa weren't even on speaking terms. Can you imagine? Over something as silly as a name?"

Annabelle giggled, realizing she was babbling inanely, but she was giddy with the knowledge that Lawrence was romantically interested in her, and she couldn't seem to control her tongue.

"However, in the end they compromised, and Father had his way," she continued. "Why, I'm probably the only woman on this ship with four names."

Amused, Lawrence smiled, his eyebrows lifting. "Oh?"

"Yes. My birth certificate reads Annabelle Christine Guinevere Mooreland," she said with a dramatic flair.

He looked at her so strangely that Annabelle blinked in confusion. Had she said something wrong? He cleared his throat. "Did you say Guinevere?"

Eyes wide, she nodded.

He continued to stare at her, the look in his eyes causing her heart to race as fast as the ship sailing across the ocean.

"Guinevere. . . ," he murmured, his tone incredulous, wondering. "I never knew. All this time. . .I never knew."

Feeling her cheeks go hot at his probing stare, she lowered her gaze. After a moment, Lawrence spoke again. "You're shivering. Perhaps we should go inside and order something hot to drink."

"Yes, that sounds like a good idea," Annabelle agreed, only part of her aware of him taking her arm and steering her toward the companionway. The other part of her wondered. . . .

❧

During dinner, a strained silence settled over the table, and Annabelle ate her meal in confusion. Her father had finally made an appearance less than an hour earlier; however, Annabelle couldn't help but be shocked at his slovenly attire, so unlike his usual impeccable grooming. His silver hair was unruly, his collar wasn't buttoned properly, his tie hung askew, and his jacket had a rumpled appearance, as if he'd slept in it.

Annabelle tried to make eye contact with him, but he avoided her numerous stares and only muttered a few abrupt words in response to her curious questions. And then there was Lawrence. . . .

Except when she asked him a question, Lawrence barely said a word. What was he thinking? Did he wish he'd never asked to call on her? Was he having second thoughts? He had mentioned something earlier about their age difference, something that had never been a concern to her. But maybe it bothered him. Maybe he had changed his mind about courting a nineteen-year-old, unable to get over the obstacle of seeing Annabelle as anything other than the child she'd been. And the way she'd foolishly chattered about her parents earlier probably hadn't helped him see her as a mature adult either.

Annabelle tried to concentrate on and enjoy her glazed roast duckling, but it was hopeless. She may as well have been eating sawdust. Feeling a bit dejected as well as rejected, she lifted her head and idly studied the diners across the spacious room. Waiters inconspicuously weaved among the tables with their large platters, offering passengers a tempting array of foods from which they could choose their next course.

Colonel Astor and his new bride, Madelaine, sat a few tables away. Sweet and dainty, she was the same age as Annabelle, though her husband looked to be in his fifties; yet *they* seemed to be happy, despite the difference in their ages. Annabelle sighed and took a sip of water. She had briefly met Madelaine earlier in the voyage, while trying to compose yet another letter in the ladies' reading and writing room, and had learned that Mrs. Astor was with child.

Annabelle's gaze wandered to the right. She noted the polite and helpful Colonel Gracie escorting three women past the doorman and out of the dining room. . .and there were Mr. and Mrs. Straus, who, after the first night of dining at the Mooreland's table, had not eaten with them again.

Annabelle's father had managed to strike up an acquaintance with Mr. Straus while visiting the smoking lounge, he'd told her, and had found that he, Mr. Straus, and Colonel Gracie all shared a fascination for talk of the American Civil War, which had taken place almost fifty years earlier.

Annabelle could hardly blame the Strauses for not wanting to eat with them, after remembering Charlotte's shocking behavior the first night. Again the Fontaneaus were not in attendance, causing Annabelle to wonder. As a matter of fact, she hadn't seen Charlotte all day, except for a glimpse of her earlier that afternoon. . . .

"Annabelle?"

She turned toward her father, wondering about the desperate tone of his voice. "Yes, Father?"

"As soon as you've finished, I'd like a word with you."

"Yes, Father. Of course."

She resumed eating, suddenly apprehensive, and at last gave up, laying down her fork and knife. Her father must have noted her action, for he pushed away from the table and helped Annabelle from her chair. She rose and noticed that her father's plate was still full, the roast sirloin and creamed carrots apparently untouched. Annabelle allowed herself a curious glance in Lawrence's direction.

He looked up from his plate and gave her a small smile, which boosted her spirits a bit. But she was still anxious concerning her father. What did he have to tell her? It obviously was something terrible, judging from his behavior. She wondered if it had to do with Aunt Christine. Had her father sent a wire today only to receive bad news in return?

Annabelle bit her lip and tried not to worry as she walked beside her father past the other diners and through the door.

When the Moorelands were almost at the exit, Lawrence set down his utensils and watched Annabelle's retreat, still a bit stunned. All day he had mulled over his talk with her. Was it merely a coincidence that he'd been searching for his Guinevere and Annabelle just happened to possess the name? *Lord, is this a sign from you? Is she the one for me? If so, then. . .*

Closing his eyes, Lawrence shook his head, disgusted with himself. He knew better than to put his trust in fleeces, as Gideon had done before he fought the army of Midianites in the book of Judges. In Old Testament days it had been acceptable to ask for miraculous signs for affirmation before proceeding with a given action. But that was before the Savior had come into the world. The Holy Spirit now lived inside Lawrence's heart and was his direct connection to the Father. Lawrence would pray about his relationship with Annabelle, as he should have done concerning Frances. If he had turned to God first instead of trying to please his parents, he could have avoided a lot of wasted years courting a woman he would never marry.

Lawrence had always thought Annabelle special. They had shared a friendship that some may have considered unusual; but he'd never connected with anyone as he had with her, despite the differences in their ages. Of course, he'd only thought of her in terms of friendship and had looked on her with eyes of brotherly love. . .that is, until a few days ago when he discovered her on board the *Titanic*. And strangely enough, except for a momentary shyness on Annabelle's part, they had bonded immediately, as if four years of separation hadn't existed between them.

Lawrence motioned a nearby waiter to the table and ordered a coffee. He had developed a taste for the drink while traveling on the *Titanic* and wondered if he would ever go back to the everyday ritual of drinking English tea.

Lawrence thanked the waiter, who set the steaming cup in front of him. He took a sip of the strong brew as he considered his life. One day he would have to return to Fairhaven; he had no choice in the matter. At some point he would become earl, and his duties lay at home. But for now he would stay in Manhattan, instead of touring the country as he'd planned to do before leaving England. And he would earnestly pray to God concerning Annabelle, starting tonight.

Lawrence drained his coffee and left the dining room, not interested in the remaining courses of his dinner. Ascending the stairs, he went to the boat deck, desiring a walk before retiring for the evening.

The frigid air took his breath away momentarily. He paused, looking down the length of the deserted deck, wondering if he should return to his stateroom for his warm, fur-lined overcoat. Before he could turn back to the door leading to the stairway, however, something at the stern caught his eye.

Annabelle? he wondered incredulously. He studied the lone woman wearing a fur coat. Staring out over the calm sea, she stood by the railing, her gloved hand holding one of many thick ropes that were attached to the waist-high ledge and traveled up to the tops of four tall smokestacks along the ship. Her back was to him, and he couldn't be certain it was her—there was little light. But it did look like Annabelle from this angle.

Hurriedly, Lawrence walked to where she stood, his steps loud on the silent deck, and he watched as she turned to face him. It was Annabelle! And it looked as if she'd been crying, though it was too dark to be sure.

"Lawrence," she breathed in a shaky whisper. "What are you doing here?"

"I might ask you the same thing," he said quietly, noting her gloved hand quickly swipe at her cheeks.

"I–I needed time to think," she stammered.

Lawrence watched her nervous movements as she began pulling at the fingers of her white gloves. "Do you need a shoulder to cry on, Little Belle?" he asked softly, applying the pet name he'd used for her when he'd offered comfort in the past.

She shook her head. "I'll be all right, Lawrence," she said in a wobbly voice that belied her words.

"Annabelle, this is Lawrence you're talking to, remember? We've known each other too long for you to expect me to believe that. Let's go somewhere warmer and discuss it. And might I be bold enough to suggest hot cocoa and macaroons if the ship has them?" he teased, hoping to get her to smile; he remembered how she'd lit into him the other day after he'd invited her to the Café Parisian for the childhood treats she'd so favored.

But she didn't smile. She only looked at him with huge, tear-filled emerald eyes, causing his heart to wrench in pain.

Gently taking her elbow, Lawrence steered her back to the companionway. Feeling her arm shake, he sincerely hoped there was something he could do to help her. He knew it wasn't only the frigid air that caused her body to tremble.

ten

Upon reaching the Palm Room, Lawrence spotted an empty table and led her to it. Immediately a steward came, and Lawrence ordered coffee, waiting until the young man had left before turning to Annabelle. "Now, what seems to be the problem?" he asked softly.

Annabelle clasped her hands in her lap and looked down at the table for a moment. Lifting her head, she anxiously met his caring gaze. "My. . .my father—" Annabelle broke off as the steward came with their coffee, her eyes nervously flicking back down to the table.

Lawrence resisted the urge to snap at the unassuming steward and made himself smile and thank him instead, before turning his gaze back to Annabelle. He watched as she took a sip of the black brew and grimaced. Either she wasn't accustomed to coffee or she didn't usually drink it black. He waited, trying to remain patient. A few silent minutes passed before he gently insisted, "Annabelle, please tell me what's bothering you."

She shut her eyes.

"Annabelle?" he prompted.

She opened her eyes and looked at him. Taking a shaky breath, she shook her head. "I've no idea where to start."

"How about the beginning? That's always the best place."

She nodded and took a sip of the strong coffee. "My father, before he met my mother, had a problem with gambling. He became a Christian shortly after he married Mother—it was Mama who introduced him to Christianity—and he gave up playing cards." She paused, then went on. "When Mother died, Father withdrew from me and everyone around him. I think at the time he even withdrew from God.

He was so unhappy, so angry.

"During these past eight years he mellowed, but was never quite the same—at least not how I remembered him to be when Mama was alive. Two years ago he took up playing cards again with his old friends at an exclusive gentlemen's club where he's a member, but I didn't really think he had a problem. Not then."

With a pang, Lawrence watched as tears again formed in her eyes, but he waited patiently for her to go on, knowing that if he interrupted now, she might not finish the story.

"This past year he became even more withdrawn from me. It was painful, but I understood the reason for his behavior. It hurt him to look at me. . . . I've been told I greatly resemble my mother," she added with a quaver in her voice. Annabelle took another quick sip of coffee, then her eyes flicked upward to intercept Lawrence's encouraging, sympathetic gaze.

"My mother came from a very wealthy family," she continued. "She was the eldest child, and when my grandparents died in a train accident, the house went to her." Annabelle bit her lip hard. "That's where we were going when we reached America."

Lawrence's dark brows raised in question. "Were?"

"My father gambled the house away in a card game the other night, along with a great deal of money," she blurted. "Almost everything we have—had—now belongs to Monsieur Fontaneau."

Lawrence inhaled sharply. Obviously embarrassed, she looked away toward the high-arched window, where a view of the dark ocean could be seen between the openings of the covered promenade.

"Father had the deed to the house. He brought all his important papers with him. You see, we didn't plan to return to England. We only went there eight years ago because everything in America reminded him of Mama, and he couldn't stand it," she explained dully. "But as you know, my uncle and Father didn't get along, even after we moved to the cottage, and months ago, Father decided it was time to move on—to return to the States.

"But now we have nowhere to go. Unless we stay with my aunt. But she's a recluse and blames Father for Mama's death—though it wasn't his fault," she added, fresh tears pooling in her eyes. "So now I've no idea what will become of us."

Annabelle felt his hand cover hers and turned to face him. Her heart began to race at the warm, almost possessive look in his eyes. She also detected a glimmer of anger in their depths, but knew it wasn't directed at her. Who, then? Her father?

"I know what Father did was wrong, but I don't blame him," she said softly, noting Lawrence's surprised expression. "You see, I understand what he was trying to do, in a way. Gambling is a sickness, a disease that makes the gambler think he can win with the next hand of cards. Father told me he was certain of his turn of luck when he put the house up for stakes. He'd already lost a great deal of money and was trying to win it all back. He was so positive he would win. . .but he didn't."

Lawrence nodded, admiring Annabelle for taking up for her father, even though she was now homeless, thanks to Edward Mooreland's stupidity. Lawrence had never gambled and didn't understand what would send a man to a card table to lose his money and eventually, in many cases, his honor. Oh, he knew there were those who won, but those cases were rare.

Several on board the ship were professional gamblers, Lawrence had heard, luring the unsuspecting to bid ever higher so that the professionals could line their pockets with the other men's wealth. But Lawrence wondered how those greedy, crafty men could spend money they'd dishonestly won and still live with their consciences? Didn't it bother them to reduce a man to nothing, to prey upon his weaknesses? What of the wives and children of the victims?

Lawrence felt Edward had been set up and that Eric was,

indeed, a card shark, and his sister probably was in cahoots with him. Though Lawrence didn't know much about the gambling world, he was fairly certain no true gentleman would agree to such high stakes. And the little he'd seen of the smooth-talking Frenchman convinced Lawrence that Eric fit the mold of a professional gambler.

"I should go to my room now," Annabelle said, looking down at his hand still covering hers. "Thank you for listening, Lawrence."

"Little Belle, do you trust me?"

She looked up, surprise evident on her face. "With my life."

He smiled. "Then please believe me when I say I will never let anything bad happen to you if I can help it. You'll never want for anything as long as I'm alive. Let's pray, Annabelle. God has the answer. Nothing is impossible where He's concerned."

She nodded and Lawrence offered a quiet prayer, asking God to show them light and lead them in the way they should go.

A few minutes later, Annabelle walked with him to her room. When they reached it, she turned to him. "Thank you again, Lawrence. Thank you for being there for me."

"Don't worry, Annabelle. We've prayed and now we need only trust the Lord to show us His direction," he said, his tone encouraging. "Will you attend worship services in the morning?"

Her brow furrowed. "I wasn't aware there were any."

"Yes, in the dining room after breakfast. May I escort you?"

"I'd like that," she said softly.

He bent over and kissed her forehead. "Good night, Annabelle."

Her heart racing, she leaned against the door after entering her room and replayed the last few moments. As if an icy gust of air had suddenly blown into the room, the warm feeling was doused as her mind stubbornly reminded her of her plight. She looked at her reflection in the oval mirror of the dresser.

Tired, fearful, anxious, excited—all these labels could be placed on the girl who looked back at her with wide green eyes.

❧

Sunday morning as Sadie helped her dress, Annabelle wondered if she should tell her maid that soon she would be out of a job. Seeing Sadie's beaming face, Annabelle decided to wait.

Remembering how cold it had been yesterday, she opted for a brown velvet skirt and long-sleeved white blouse, attaching her mother's cameo to the shirred high neck.

Strangely, in the quiet hours of the night, Annabelle had come to accept her fate with a calm that surprised her. Whether Aunt Christine allowed her homeless brother-in-law and niece to come live with her wasn't an issue to Annabelle any longer. If her aunt didn't offer her home to them, Annabelle had already decided what she would do.

Although she was grateful for Lawrence's offer of help, she couldn't accept monetary assistance from him. It wouldn't be proper, even though they were good friends.

Her father didn't tell her how much money he'd lost, but Annabelle assumed it was a great deal if he'd needed to put the house up for stakes. They might be practically destitute. She was thankful her stateroom was paid for in advance. At least she wouldn't be kicked out of it. But upon reaching America they would need money soon, she was certain, and her father wasn't as young as he used to be. He may not like the idea of her working, but Annabelle felt certain there was some position she could acquire that he'd look on as acceptable. Perhaps Mrs. Brown—*Maggie,* Annabelle silently corrected herself—would know.

Annabelle pulled on white gloves and pinned a wide-brimmed hat loaded with russet flowers to the top of her head. Her gaze went to the velvet-lined jewelry box sitting on the dresser.

Every year on her birthday and at Christmas—starting when Annabelle turned fourteen—her father had given her a piece of her mother's jewelry. And Annabelle treasured each gift. Each time she wore the jewelry, Annabelle felt close to the woman whom she'd known such a short time. Though the gems would probably bring a small fortune, there was no way Annabelle felt she could part with them, selfish as that made her feel. At least not yet.

Resisting the urge to cry, she turned to her maid and held her arms out from her sides. "Well, Sadie, what do you think?"

"Oh, Miss Annabelle—you're truly a vision, you are. Why, I'm certain you'll be the envy of every woman who sees you."

Annabelle smiled. "Well, I'm not certain I want that, but thank you for the compliment, Sadie. You may go now."

Sadie bobbed a curtsey, though Annabelle wasn't royalty. But when her maid did that it made Annabelle feel special—just like when Lawrence stared at her with his icy-warm eyes. . . .

"He's no longer for you, so stop this nonsense right now!" Annabelle said sharply to the dreamy-eyed girl in the mirror. "You could hardly allow Lawrence to court a penniless, homeless waif! Especially after the experience he had with Frances."

Turning away from the plea she saw in the green eyes, Annabelle hurried to the other side of the room to snatch her shawl from the trunk.

❧

Annabelle curiously looked at her father over her glass, still surprised he had asked her to join him early in his stateroom for a light breakfast of fruit and scones. From the despairing way he'd acted when she'd last seen him, Annabelle had thought her father would spend the rest of the voyage isolated from everyone, including her. Today his appearance was much cleaner, neater, though there was still a look of hopelessness in his eyes. She set down her juice and covered his hand with her own. He looked at her, obviously surprised and a little anxious.

"Father, I want you to know I forgive you for losing the house. We'll get by."

The ghost of a smile he managed was hardly encouraging, but Annabelle refused to again fall into the pit of misery she'd wallowed in most of last night. Like Christian in the Slough of Despond in *The Pilgrim's Progress*. Or David, when he'd been a fugitive fleeing from Saul's wrath. It had taken hours of prayer and poring over the Psalms to regain hope; but like King David, she, too, had cried out to God, knowing that somehow, some way, He would help her.

"You're a good girl, Annabelle. No man could have a finer daughter," Edward said, his eyes lowering from her steady gaze.

"And I'm glad you're my father." He gave a snort of disbelief, and she nodded briskly. "I mean that; you're a good man. Mama must have thought you were very special, too. She loved you very much; I remember that."

At the mention of Cynthia, Edward's expression softened, then took on a guilty look. "I've failed your mother," he said before looking away.

"Nonsense," Annabelle was quick to reply. "You made a mistake—everyone makes mistakes. But you know how easy it is to be forgiven. . . ." She paused, until his eyes again flicked to hers. "Come to church services with me today. Please."

Edward hesitated. It had been a long time since he'd gone to church. Not since God took his Cynthia away. . . .

"Please, My Papa."

Upon hearing the endearing term she had used as a little girl, Edward felt a touch of nostalgia, and his eyes misted. "Your mother would be proud if she could see you now," he said softly.

The cameo Annabelle wore at her neck was the one Cynthia had worn when Edward first met her. Oh, she had been a beauty! Except for Annabelle's dark hair and a few other details, it was almost as if his wife were here with him now. He closed his eyes, willing himself to return to reality.

"Father?"

Seeing the pleading, expectant look on her face, he knew he couldn't refuse; he owed her this favor and so much more besides. "All right, Annabelle. I'll come to church with you."

She squeezed his hand, and they both smiled.

Her heart felt infinitely lighter, and she silently thanked God for this breakthrough.

eleven

As Annabelle entered the dining room on her father's arm, she studied the people gathered for the worship service. She was looking for a certain face. He was already there, as she knew he would be. But there wasn't time to talk now; she and her father were late, arriving just as the service began. It had been worth it, though. They had talked—*really talked*—about so many things. Never could Annabelle remember a time when she and her father had been closer.

Annabelle turned to number 418 in her hymnal. A warm feeling filled her when she looked down at the words and sang, her husky alto blending with the other voices. She closed her eyes, letting the encouraging words of Isaac Watts minister to her spirit. She knew God would take care of her; God would find them a home. He would help her no matter what life might bring. Boldly she sang the last verses:

Before the hills in order stood,
Or earth received her frame
From everlasting Thou art God,
To endless years the same.
A thousand ages in Thy sight,
Are like an evening gone
Short as the watch that ends the night,
Before the rising sun.
Time like an ever-rolling stream,
Bears all her song away
They fly forgotten as the dream,
Dies at the opening day.
O God our help in ages past,
Our hope for years to come

Be Thou our guide while life shall last,
And our eternal home.

Afterward, Annabelle felt as if the warm breath of God had blown over her, comforting her, reassuring her. For her, the song alone made the service worthwhile. It was exactly what she needed to hear, confirming everything she'd read in the book of Psalms.

Feelings of doubt had crept in this past hour. Like the man Christian, trapped in Doubting Castle, Annabelle had begun to worry about what was in store for them. But the hymn acted like the promised key to open the door and free her from her dark prison of uncertainty. God was omnipotent; He had a place for them to live and a future for them to enjoy. She would trust Him to lead and protect her, just as the Psalms said He would.

Annabelle tried to concentrate on Captain Smith's message, but with her peripheral vision she could see Lawrence's puzzled gaze upon her. She hadn't been kind to him, she knew that. She had agreed to let him escort her to the service and then she hadn't been there when he came to pick her up. And he probably wondered where she'd been during breakfast as well. It hadn't been her idea to eat in her father's stateroom, but she was glad they had. If they hadn't sought privacy, they might not have talked about personal matters, and her father might not be sitting next to her now.

She stole a glance at her father and noted his erect posture and his intent expression as he listened, tears in his eyes.

It had been a mistake to look at her father, Annabelle realized, for suddenly her eyes cut to Lawrence and his gaze caught hers, trapping her. Tingles raced up and down her arms and her cheeks grew warm. He gave her an uncertain smile. She managed to smile back, then quickly faced the front, focusing on the commanding figure of Captain Smith. But no matter how hard she tried to concentrate on his words, thoughts of the man sitting a few chairs away kept invading her mind.

After the service was over, Annabelle felt guilty that she didn't even know the subject of the captain's message. She determined that she would read several extra chapters in her Bible to make up for her lack of concentration this morning.

As she had known he would, once the people were dismissed, Lawrence quickly came to her side. "Hello, Annabelle."

"Hello."

"I missed you this morning."

Annabelle looked to her father, who'd spotted Colonel Gracie and was now talking to him. "Father and I had breakfast in his stateroom," she explained. "We had much to discuss."

Lawrence nodded. "Would you care to take a walk with me?"

"No, I don't think so. It's much too cold." And it was. Annabelle had risen early to view the sunrise, but upon arriving on the boat deck, had decided against it. Maybe tomorrow.

"Annabelle—"

"Oh, there's Mrs. Brown!" Annabelle interrupted. "Won't you please excuse me, Lawrence? I'm sorry, but I really must ask her something. I'll talk to you later." She hated to be rude, but she really needed to talk with Maggie. As she hurried away—her mind imprinted with the surprised, hurt, and confused look on his face—Annabelle managed to paste on a smile and greet her friend. "Hello, Maggie!"

"Well, I do declare. Don't you look like a bright ray of warm sunshine on this cold mornin'," Maggie said with a smile when Annabelle stopped in front of her. Her dark eyes cut to the tall man in the background, wistfully looking in their direction. "Isn't that your nice young man?"

Annabelle couldn't help the flush that she felt warming her face. However, she chose to ignore Maggie's question. "I really need some advice about something. Could you help me, Maggie?"

The woman didn't hesitate, but nodded and steered Annabelle toward the lift. "I need warmin' up. Let's go fetch us a cup o' tea, and then we'll talk."

Once they were seated at one of the tables in the Café Parisian and had given their order to the young stewardess, Maggie turned to Annabelle. "Now how can I help, honey?"

Annabelle hesitated, wondering if she was doing the right thing by confiding in someone that she hardly knew. "I have a bit of a problem," she explained. "I may need to look for work when we reach America, but I don't know what sort of jobs are available—or acceptable—for a woman. I–I wouldn't bother you with this, but I don't know who else to ask." Annabelle's gaze lowered to her clasped hands on the table in front of her.

"Why do you need to look for work?" Maggie asked.

Annabelle's face grew warm. "It seems that. . .well, the fact is. . ." She broke off, embarrassed, unable to continue.

Maggie reached over and patted her clasped hands. "That's all right. You don't have to talk about it if you don't want to." There was a small pause. "Let's see. . .about your question. Hmmm. A governess position is respectable, or a teacher—but I think you have to have a certificate to do that. . . ."

Annabelle's heart grew heavy as Maggie ticked off different occupations on the fingers of one hand. It seemed, according to Maggie, that one either had to have special schooling, or credentials, or references, or a certificate, or *something* Annabelle didn't have.

Later, in her room, she sat staring out the porthole, her Bible open in her lap. She'd considered her plight. She wished she had some kind of talent, like the unknown woman who'd made the lovely blanket. But Annabelle had never excelled at embroidery, sewing, drawing, or painting. Not like Patricia had.

Patricia had been gifted with probably every artistic ability in existence. She was even an accomplished musician, playing the harp. Annabelle had tried learning to play the piano once, but her uncle soon put a stop to that, tiring of all the jarring, discordant notes she banged out.

A knock at the door interrupted her musings, and Annabelle

turned her head sharply at the unexpected sound, bidding entrance. Sadie walked in. "Sorry to interrupt, miss, but I. . ." She lowered her head.

"Yes, Sadie?" Annabelle asked, puzzled by the strange way her maid was acting.

Sadie raised bright eyes and looked directly at her. "The fact is, Miss Annabelle, I have something important to discuss, and I wanted to speak with you first, before I talked to Mr. Mooreland." She fidgeted, shifting from one foot to the other. "You see, miss, I met a nice young man. . . . Well, the truth of the matter is, he, uh. . .he asked me to marry him."

Annabelle's eyes grew round, and she drew in her breath swiftly. "Sadie, I don't know what to say. . . . How long have you known him?" she asked, suddenly realizing the stupidity of such a question. It couldn't have been long; this was only their fifth day on the *Titanic*.

Sadie began to wring her hands. "I met Hans the day we boarded. He brought things to my door when I was sick—he's a steward on the ship—and we started talking. Later, after I got better, I spent more time with him when he was off duty."

Seeing Annabelle's skeptical gaze, Sadie hastened to say, "Oh, Hans is a good, kind Christian man, miss! We attended church services in second class this morning—he was off duty—and he proposed right afterward.

"You should see him, miss. He's tall and blond and has the most dreamy blue eyes—like the ocean, they are. . . ."

Annabelle sighed. "And you love him."

Sadie hesitated, then nodded.

"Sadie, I can't tell you what to do concerning your personal life, but five days isn't a great deal of time to acquaint yourself with anyone. Especially someone you think you may want to marry!"

Sadie bit her lip and nodded. "Yes, miss. I'll think on it more." She looked down, uncomfortable, then up again. "I want you to know, miss, I've enjoyed being in your employ.

And if I do decide to marry Hans. . .I'll–I'll greatly miss you."

Annabelle felt the tears prick her eyelids. Sadie had been with her for almost four years—ever since her father had decided she was no longer a child and needed a personal maid.

"I'll miss you too, Sadie."

Sadie nodded and brushed away a stray tear. "If there's nothing you need me for, Miss Annabelle, then I'll leave. I'll be back at six o'clock to help you dress for dinner."

Annabelle smiled and assured her that she would be fine. As she watched Sadie's slim form disappear through the door, a fleeting thought went through her head. *Well, that would take care of the problem of having to let Sadie go.*

Actually, Annabelle hoped it would all work out for Sadie, and that her young man was everything she thought him to be. Remembering the sparkle in her maid's eyes, Annabelle was glad Sadie had found love. Lawrence's handsome face materialized in Annabelle's mind and she closed her Bible a little more forcefully than she had intended.

Perhaps a walk on the covered promenade would help her to think of other things. She must resign herself to the fact that there could never be a future for them together now.

Annabelle reached the grand staircase and spotted her father at the same time he caught sight of her. After excusing himself from the bearded gentleman with whom he was conversing, he walked her way. "Annabelle! I thought you'd retired to your room."

"I tried, but I'm restless. I can't seem to concentrate on the Scriptures today," she said, happy to see a marked improvement in her father's carriage and expression. "I thought I'd take a walk on the promenade. Would you like to join me, Father?"

"No, dear. It's much too cold for my old bones."

"Oh, Father. You're hardly old and decrepit yet," she said with a smile. "But I do understand your abhorrence of the cold. The temperature has dropped sharply since we boarded." Something suddenly occurred to her. "Have you contacted Aunt Christine?"

"Blast it all—no, I haven't. I suppose I should wire her and tell her of my folly and ask if we might stay there for a time. . . ," he said, adding a defeated sigh. "I'll go right now and do so. Don't worry, Annabelle. There's still plenty of time before we reach America."

❧

Edward walked to the boat deck, wishing he'd worn his long overcoat before braving the elements. The sea was flat as a sheet of glass, which, according to one of his well-traveled scientific comrades, was unusual.

According to his friend, the winter had been characterized by storms that regularly whipped the seas into a frenzy; its placid appearance now was quite uncommon. He also had told Edward he'd heard that other ships had telegraphed reports of iceberg sightings in the area, which was strange because they usually didn't float this far south.

Edward mentally shrugged, not all that concerned, and his mind switched gears. What would they do upon reaching America? Could he find work when he wasn't qualified for anything, having been raised to a life of wealth and luxury as the youngest son of a shipping magnate? At least he knew Annabelle would be taken care of, come her twenty-first birthday, thanks to Cynthia's parents. But what about until then? He supposed they would have to move in with Christine. That is, if she would let them. He wished Cynthia were here to advise him of what to do. Of course, if she were here, none of this ever would have happened.

Stop it right now! Face up to your own guilt and stop trying to blame others, he harshly told himself.

Cynthia had so wanted another baby—though the doctor had warned her it would be dangerous—and she had died happy, not knowing her son would follow his mother a few hours later. Edward supposed he should be thankful for that, anyway; baby

Henry hadn't died before his mother, causing Cynthia grief.

It had helped to go to church with Annabelle. In that brief hour, Edward had felt convicted concerning his behavior these past years, and he had felt God's love warming his heart, urging him to forgive, to let go.

But still he held back. All these years, he thought he'd blamed God; but now Edward realized it was really himself he blamed—he'd welcomed the chance to have a son, despite the doctor's dire warnings after Annabelle had been born. Perhaps Christine was right; perhaps he *had* killed Cynthia. . . .

An officer hurried over to him, his cheeks red from the cold. "Something I can help you with, sir?"

Edward forced his mind off the past. "Yes. I need some directions. I want to send a wireless."

"I'm sorry, sir, but the radio broke down about an hour ago. The chief operator has assured us it will be working again, soon, though. May I suggest you try again this evening?"

Frustrated, Edward gave a vague nod. He should have sent the wire yesterday, as he'd told Annabelle he would. But he'd been too busy wallowing in self-pity.

After thanking the young man, Edward hurried back down the companionway, intent on ordering a cup of hot beef broth. He would try again later.

twelve

Annabelle pulled her fur coat closer as she walked along the covered promenade. Few people were about, having more sense than to be out in the freezing cold, but Annabelle didn't care. She needed privacy, needed to be away from all the noise and confusion. There were decisions to be made. . .a future to plan.

She toyed with the idea of offering her services to her aunt. She could be a companion to the old woman, give her medicine when she needed it—if she needed it. Aunt Christine was a bit of a hypochondriac, always believing she was suffering from the latest ailment present in Newark at a given time. Ninety-nine percent of the time she wasn't.

Annabelle sighed, pulled her fur collar closer around her ears, and looked at the calm ocean. The sun shone off a glimmer of white far away on the horizon. She stepped closer to the opening of the promenade, craning her neck to see. An iceberg?

Annabelle had never seen one, but would like to. Sadie had told her that she'd spotted an iceberg floating by her porthole window the previous night. However, what Annabelle was seeing, or trying to see, was too far away. Probably a mirage (did they have those at sea?) or a trick of sunlight on water. A shiver ran down her back, and she decided it was high time to return to her cabin. The temperature must have dropped several degrees just in the few minutes she'd been out here.

Annabelle had just reached the corridor to her stateroom when an annoying, familiar voice stopped her. "Miss Mooreland! Please wait one moment; I would like to have a word wiz you."

Annabelle halted, wishing she could flee down the hallway

to her room and escape an unwanted conversation. However, against her better judgment, she waited for the redhead to approach. "Hello, Mademoiselle Fontaneau. I was just going to my room. I'm rather tired," Annabelle tried politely.

She thought she detected a look of alarm in the cat green eyes, but wasn't certain. It had passed so quickly. "Oh, please wait one moment. I would like to talk wiz you about somezing important." Charlotte twisted her slender fingers in agitation.

Annabelle hesitated. The woman did look distressed, almost. . .desperate? Terrified? But why? "Very well, mademoiselle. What did you wish to say?"

Charlotte cast a quick look down the corridor. "Oh, please, not here in ze hallway. Someone may hear."

Annabelle sighed, growing a little impatient. "What would you suggest, then?"

Charlotte pointed to a stateroom door a few yards away. "Zat is my stateroom. Let us go zere—eet is more private. I promise, I will only take a few minutes of your time."

Annabelle grudgingly nodded. She didn't want to spend any more time than she had to with a woman like Charlotte Fontaneau, but curiosity overrode common sense. Annabelle followed her into the room, idly taking note of the furniture and decorations. French Provincial—what else? Even the colors of the décor fit Charlotte. Olive greens, muted golds, and rich creams.

Charlotte motioned to a chair, and Annabelle obediently sat down, waiting. Charlotte began to slowly pace, smoothing her fiery hair, wringing her ivory hands. "Miss Mooreland, I. . ." She broke off and turned, looking straight at Annabelle. "I want to apologize for what Eric did to your papa. I had no idea he would do such a zing. You must believe me."

Annabelle shrugged, and Charlotte seemed to wilt.

"I know you do not care for me. And I can understand why." She turned and took a few steps toward the porthole, her gaze focusing on the sea beyond. "I wish we could have been friends," she said so softly that Annabelle almost didn't hear her.

Charlotte gave a despairing sigh, causing Annabelle to feel a bit of grudging sympathy. Looking at the woman, Annabelle saw traces of unhappiness clearly marked on her face. Had they always been there? Annabelle had never taken the time to notice before. Feeling as if she should say something, she cleared her throat. "I don't blame you for what happened to my father. He's a grown man who knew better than to do what he did. But sometimes he makes stupid mistakes. We *all* do."

Green eyes wide, Charlotte turned to her. "But how can you be so–so forgiving, so unconcerned? You have lost your home."

Annabelle nodded sadly, but her reply came firm. "Yes, that's true. However, I have the assurance that God will take care of me and will find me a new home. It's only because He's a part of my life that I'm able to survive this calamity. Without Him, I would be reduced to a quivering, frightened child—and at first I was, I'll admit. But now, I'm no longer afraid."

Sinking into the chair across from her, Charlotte looked intently at Annabelle. "You are good—a lady. But not all people are good." A flush of rose tinted her cheeks. "Some people are very bad and God wants nuzing to do wiz zem. If someone like zis has troubles, what can zey do? Tell me, what hope do zey have?"

Annabelle thoughtfully studied Charlotte, and suddenly words seemed to pour from her mouth that she knew weren't her own. "In the first place, you're wrong about God not wanting to have anything to do with those people," she said softly. "It is His desire that all come to know Him. He sent His Son Jesus to die for the sinners, not for the saints."

At Charlotte's look of surprise, Annabelle continued. "It's true. He knew it was impossible for man to keep all the laws of Moses. So He sent His Son to redeem us so that everyone who comes to know Him is under grace and no longer under the law, which leads to death."

"Does zat mean, zen, it is all right to have sin in one's life?" Charlotte asked, incredulous, yet hopeful.

"Of course not! It means His blood can wash us clean from the sins we commit. The Bible tells us 'all have sinned and come short of the glory of God.' Only by accepting Jesus and what He did for us on the cross can we be set free."

Charlotte's head lowered despondently. "But what if someone is born wiz ze sin and it can never go away, no matter how much zey want it to?" she whispered.

"What are you talking about?" Annabelle studied her, perplexed. "The blood of Jesus washes *all* sins away."

Charlotte opened her mouth to speak but was interrupted by a loud knock at the door. Her eyes widened, and Annabelle thought she detected fear in their depths. An immediate change came over the woman—her manner now panicked, yet commanding—as she suddenly leaned across the table toward Annabelle.

"Miss Mooreland," Charlotte said softly, quickly. "I must warn you. Stay away from Eric—he is an evil man."

Baffled, Annabelle watched as Charlotte then turned and walked to the door, opening it. Eric walked inside, his dark blue eyes instantly lighting on Annabelle. "Good afternoon, Miss Mooreland. What an unexpected pleasure to find you here," he said smoothly. "I've seen so little of you since we've boarded. Perhaps, later, you would care to take lunch wiz me?"

Annabelle gave him an incredulous look. Did he actually think after what he'd done to her father—to her—that she would desire to spend time in his company? And yet. . .perhaps she could sway him to forget the debt her father owed and allow them to keep the house. Were such things done? Judging from his elegant dress and grooming, as well as that of his sister's, he had plenty of wealth. Would he listen to Annabelle if she pleaded with him?

Annabelle looked into the frightened, warning eyes of

Charlotte, who stood behind him, and then her eyes cut to his. Beyond their dark-blue color, Annabelle sensed hardness, ruthlessness, and yes. . .evil.

Annabelle shivered, instinctively realizing he might do as she asked, but he would expect a far greater price in return—something she wasn't willing to give. What intuition told her this, she wasn't certain; perhaps it was the Lord gently warning her. She knew she must heed the voice, leave this place, and seek the safety of her room as soon as possible. She rose from the chair. "I'm sorry, Monsieur Fontaneau, but I don't feel well. I think I'll return to my room now and lie down."

"Perhaps later—"

"No, I don't think so. I have plans for later in the evening. If you'll excuse me?" Annabelle said as she quickly walked past him and to the door. Without waiting for a reply, she made her escape and hurried down the corridor to her room, not relaxing until she was inside and had locked her door.

On shaky legs she walked over to the bed and sank down upon the satin coverlet. Grabbing up the pillow from underneath the bedspread, she held it close and prayed to God for protection. She wouldn't feel safe until this voyage was over and Monsieur Fontaneau was out of her life for good.

Lawrence's face came to mind, and for a brief, wonderful moment, Annabelle dreamed of a future with him. "But no," she told herself for probably the hundredth time since he'd left her at her door last night, "it's impossible. Totally impossible."

Annabelle tossed the pillow aside. Perhaps it would be better if she avoided him for the rest of the voyage rather than put herself through this misery. Up until a few days ago, she'd never thought a future between them could be possible anyway. So maybe she could blot out the brief time they'd shared when he'd looked at her with eyes filled with something more than friendship. She would get over him. . .eventually. Besides, soon he would return to England to take over the family duties, and she would remain in America. And she'd always have her cherished memories of their years together, when Lawrence had been her dearest friend. No one could ever take that away.

Annabelle sighed and picked up the pillow again, burying her face in its softness and allowing her tears to wet it. "Oh, God, please help me get through this," she cried softly. "I'm alone again, always alone. And I've always been so afraid to be alone! That's one reason I wanted to marry Roger. But You already knew that, didn't You? I suppose I wasn't fair to him either. He wasn't the only one in the wrong. Forgive me, Lord.

"I turned my back on Your will and agreed to marry someone who didn't know You so I could attain popularity and the worldly pleasures of this life! But after losing almost everything, I realize earth's riches are fleeting. Please forgive my vanity, Lord. . .and help me to release Lawrence. I'll always love him, but I know he's no longer for me. Perhaps he never was. Maybe I'm destined to remain alone forever. Please give me the grace to accept my lot in life." She sighed and raised her head to look at the gilded walls.

My child, you are never alone. I am with you always—even until the end of time. . . . I will never leave you nor forsake you. Nothing can pluck you from my Father's hand, and nothing can ever separate you from My steadfast love. . . .

As the soothing voice spoke deep within her parched spirit, bringing forth its living waters, Annabelle felt ten times lighter—though she now had no home, no money, and no chance of a relationship with Lawrence. It defied human reasoning, but Annabelle felt a sweet peace.

❧

A few hours later the warm glow had faded somewhat, but the fear hadn't returned. However, Annabelle knew she must steer clear of Lawrence. It wouldn't be fair to him to do otherwise. She'd been selfish this past year in agreeing to marry Roger when she knew it was wrong to do so, and she wouldn't think of her own interests again—especially when it concerned someone she loved. Lawrence needed so much more than she could ever give him.

Annabelle walked to the ladies' reading and writing room, *The Pilgrim's Progress* in hand, and noted that there weren't any empty chairs. She sighed. Perhaps in the lounge.

But even the lounge was full. However, Annabelle spotted an empty chair near the window and made a beeline for it. She supposed the bitter cold outside had something to do with the crowded rooms. She sank onto the comfortable chair and opened her book. But the steady hum of voices floating around the room was distracting, and she finally closed the book, having read only two paragraphs in fifteen minutes.

Annabelle glanced around the room, observing those about her. Men and women sat talking, reading, drinking coffee and tea, and generally having a good time, judging from the smiles and soft laughter. Annabelle's heart seemed to stop as she saw Lawrence walk through the door.

Quickly she opened the book and lifted it to eye-level, shielding her face and hoping he wouldn't notice her. She wasn't ready to deal with him just yet.

"Annabelle?"

She swallowed hard and lowered the book, finding him standing directly in front of her. Her heart gave a little jump.

"Oh. Hello," she said, wishing her voice didn't sound so strange. At least there were no available chairs nearby.

Almost as though he'd heard her thought and wanted to provoke her, the elderly man in the next chair closed his book, checked his gold watch dangling from its fob, then slipped the timepiece back into the pocket of his silk vest and abruptly rose. Lawrence immediately sat down and turned to face her.

"How has your day been?" he asked.

"Fine, thanks."

"A bit cold, though."

"Yes, it has been." She fidgeted with her book.

"The temperature is dropping even as we speak."

"Really?"

"Yes. I'd advise you to dress warmly tonight."

"Thank you, I will." Annabelle bit the inside of her lip, uncomfortable with this inane conversation, even more uncomfortable to have him sitting so close. "If you'll excuse me, I think I'll go to my stateroom for a bit of a rest."

She rose and almost succeeded in walking away, but suddenly felt the searing heat of Lawrence's hand as he grasped her wrist, stopping her. She turned her head and looked at him, shocked.

"Annabelle, have I done something to offend you?"

Shame coursed through her when she heard the puzzled tone in his voice. "No, of course not," she assured him.

"Then why are you avoiding me?" he asked bluntly.

She bit the inside of her lip, knowing she had to tell him. He deserved the truth. . .but not right now. She needed time to think and pray, time to formulate her thoughts and plan what to say to him. She needed time to compose herself, to be in total control of her feelings; it simply wouldn't do for her to break down and cry—as she wanted to do at this moment.

"Lawrence, I know I've behaved rudely, and I'm sorry. Tonight, after dinner, we'll talk then. I really must go now," Annabelle said softly, so those nearby wouldn't hear.

He nodded, his eyes seeming to melt her, as he released her wrist. "All right, Annabelle. I intend to hold you to it."

Annabelle turned and hurried away, wondering how she would ever get through this night.

❧

Lawrence watched Annabelle hurry across the patterned carpet, her velvet dress swishing around her ankles. Why was she suddenly so distant toward him? Lawrence knew the events of yesterday weighed heavily on her mind. However, before, they'd always been able to talk to one another, to confide in each other, but for some reason she was now shutting him out.

He had prayed long into the evening last night, getting

only two hours of sleep. But he'd prayed until he believed the Lord had clearly shown him an answer, and he planned to seek out Edward Mooreland tonight and discuss it with him.

The idea of a lifetime with Annabelle gave nothing but great pleasure to Lawrence, and he wondered just when it was he'd begun to deeply love her. Perhaps subconsciously he'd always had strong feelings for her and had known that one day she would be his. Maybe that's why the idea of an engagement to Frances, or any of the other young ladies he'd met, had never appealed.

Of course, he would spend the required amount of time courting Annabelle, and later he'd propose. They would marry and return to Fairview, where his mother could train Annabelle on what was expected of a viscountess. They would raise their children in the English countryside, where generations of Caldwells had been born, and they would remain best friends all the days of their lives and grow old together. . . . He smiled, staring at nothing in particular, imagining how Annabelle would look as a bride. . . .

Lawrence sighed. He was putting the apple cart ahead of the horse again, as his nanny used to tell him. Before he planned their entire future, he ought to tell Annabelle how he felt and make certain she returned his feelings. Then, too, remembering her independent streak, he didn't think she'd be too thrilled about Lawrence leaving her out of the plans he was busily making for them. But he hoped to remedy that situation very soon.

thirteen

Annabelle randomly selected a necklace with onyx and diamonds embedded in its elaborate setting and fastened it around her neck. Usually she rifled through the jewel box, trying on one piece of her mother's jewelry after another, holding them against her throat, studying, deliberating until she reached a decision. But tonight her mind was far away.

She looked into the mirror. True, the necklace she selected matched, but it was rather much to wear over the detailed velvet gown with the wide silver lace running along its square neckline.

Blowing out a breath of frustration, Annabelle snatched the necklace from around her neck and threw it back into the box. "Oh, I don't know what's wrong with me tonight, Sadie! I can't seem to think clearly."

"If I may suggest, miss. . ." Sadie pawed through the velvet interior of the ornate silver box. "I think this will complement the blue-gray of the gown quite well."

Annabelle took the simple silver necklace interspersed with tiny dark-blue sapphires and held it up to her throat. "Yes, Sadie, I think you're right," she said, relieved. "Please fasten it for me; the catch is too small."

Annabelle studied her reflection in the mirror while her maid fastened the necklace. Her face was too pale. Because she'd inherited the creamy white skin and rosy cheeks of her Irish grandmother, she usually never bothered with cosmetics, except for a dab of rice powder on her nose and lip rouge for her mouth. But tonight she definitely needed something!

Annabelle selected a pot of lip rouge, popped off the cap, and then to Sadie's obvious shock, judging from her expression in the mirror, dipped her finger and dabbed colored circles on her cheeks. She tried to blend the color into her skin, but the effect was hideous. She ended up with bold red blotches on either side of her white face. "Oh, Sadie! Go get me a washcloth! And hurry," she cried in horror.

Sadie left, and Annabelle clutched the top of the vanity. Vain—yes, that's what she'd been. Why did it matter how she looked? Soon she would tell Lawrence of her decision not to see him anymore and why. She knew he'd likely offer protests, but in the end he'd see it was for the best, and they would part with fond memories. She looked in the mirror sadly; their romance was over before it had even begun.

Annabelle's wistful expression turned into one of relief as Sadie walked in, bearing a wet washcloth. Annabelle took it gratefully and scrubbed it across her cheeks. The streaks were gone, but now she looked even more like a clown.

"Oh, Sadie, what am I going to do?"

Sadie studied her thoughtfully, then reached for the rice powder and opened the lid of the canister.

"Of course! Why didn't I think of that?" Annabelle took the puff, dipped it into the chalky powder, then swished it over her cheeks. The ending result was better, but still Annabelle wished she had let well enough alone in the first place.

A knock on the door interrupted her perusal. "Well, I'm ready, and just in time—there's Father. Please let him in, and then put the jewelry back in the safe after we've gone."

Annabelle scanned the room for her mother's silver lace fan with the little mirror in the middle. Finding it, she snatched it up and turned toward the door. "Lawrence!"

He stood on the threshold behind Sadie and smiled at Annabelle. He looked so handsome in his black silk evening clothes and white bow tie; the sight momentarily took her breath away. "I asked permission of your father to escort you to dinner tonight," he explained softly.

She held out her arm to him in a daze, and Lawrence took her hand and placed it in the crook of his arm. It was impossible not to notice how she trembled, and he turned his head and looked down at her, giving her an encouraging smile.

Annabelle felt as if she were in a dream as she walked down the carpeted corridor to the grand staircase with Lawrence as her escort. This wasn't supposed to be happening! How was she to maintain any kind of distance with him when her hand was wrapped around his arm and he walked so close? She was more than a little aware of his muscular strength and his vitality, and it made her want to melt against him. She put space between them and almost bumped into a couple just walking out of their stateroom.

"Careful," Lawrence warned as he gently tugged on her arm, bringing her back closer, to avert a collision.

They headed for the lift. Annabelle knew it would be sweet torture to be alone with him in such a confined space, but the lift was faster than the stairs, and so they would reach their destination that much sooner, she assured herself.

The lift was confined, but they weren't alone, as two other couples and a small child walked on at the last moment. Annabelle held her breath as Lawrence drew her closer to him to make room for the others.

"Are you not feeling well?" he asked in concern when the man working the lift pulled back the grilled gate upon reaching D-deck, and they walked out into the spacious room. Annabelle never thought she would be so glad to see wide-open spaces with plenty of room to walk.

"I–I'm fine," she said while briskly fanning her face. "I think I just need to sit down."

Lawrence took her arm and led her past the beveled glass door into the dining room. American beauty roses and white daisies in crystal vases were in abundance throughout the room, their sweet aroma filling the air. Her father already sat at one of the covered tables, next to two empty seats usually occupied by the Fontaneaus.

I hope Charlotte is well. The automatic thought surprised Annabelle, especially when she realized she meant it. Something had happened earlier in the day in Charlotte's stateroom, causing the animosity Annabelle felt toward the woman to flee. Perhaps it was the hopelessness, the yearning Annabelle had seen in Charlotte's eyes when Annabelle told her about God's love and mercy.

Annabelle had seen a side of Charlotte she hadn't even known existed. Gone had been the flirtatious, happy, sometimes tipsy woman, and in her place had sat a frightened little girl, anxious to be loved and accepted—yet sadly resigned to the idea she never could be. Especially by God. *What happened in Charlotte's life to make her feel that way?* Annabelle wondered as she sat next to her father.

She bowed her head to say grace quietly, as she always did, and was surprised when her father's large hand covered hers. Stunned, she looked at him and noted that he, too, had bowed his head. Annabelle felt as if a small ray of sunshine had brightened the gloom, and again she silently thanked God that her father had attended the worship service with her.

The three tried to do justice to the sumptuous eleven-course dinner, but they had too much on their minds to partake in most of the tempting dishes served or to engage in anything but trivial conversation. After dessert was served and sparingly eaten, Lawrence turned to Annabelle, his eyes hopeful, expectant. "I believe we have something to discuss."

Annabelle suddenly felt as if furry caterpillars were crawling in her stomach. She took a quick sip of tea, hoping it would help. It didn't. Nervously, she nodded to her father before walking away with Lawrence.

❧

Edward thoughtfully watched as Lord Caldwell escorted Annabelle away from the table and to the door. He would make a good husband for his daughter. Edward liked the young man and, in the eight years he had known Lawrence, believed him to be dependable, responsible, and a true gentleman. And most importantly—he was a man in love with his daughter.

That fact had been obvious when Lawrence had visited him

in the smoking lounge earlier and had asked Edward's permission to court and eventually wed Annabelle, if she would have him. Edward wasn't blind and could see Lawrence was sincere in his love for Annabelle. Much as Edward had felt about Cynthia.

He sighed, picked up his spoon, and finished his Waldorf pudding. At least he would rest easier, knowing Annabelle would be well taken care of, come what may. He only hoped his daughter had enough sense to say "yes" to Lawrence's proposal.

❧

Dreading the next few minutes, Annabelle walked beside Lawrence along the covered promenade to the Palm Room, and distinctly felt the sharp chill in the air. She was relieved to arrive in the warm, brightly lit room and hear the ship's band playing next door. Now there would be less chance of her and Lawrence being overheard by others.

Lawrence ordered them coffee, and this time Annabelle made it a point to add sugar and cream to hers, remembering the bitter brew from the previous night. She idly listened to a few notes of the bouncy ragtime song the musicians played, while wondering how to begin with what she had to say.

"Annabelle? I have something I need to discuss with you. . . ."

"No, Lawrence, please let me speak first," she pleaded. "I–I want you to know I've enjoyed knowing you—the times we shared in England, the talks we had, the Bible studies, the stories you read to me, everything. And being with you again these past few days has been wonderful. I shall always hold the memories dear to my heart," she choked. Her gaze lowered to her cup. She stared at the brown liquid as if she'd never seen it before.

Lawrence stiffened. "This sounds a lot like a good-bye," he joked, intently studying her bent head.

"It is."

His brows drew down into a frown. "Annabelle, I—"

"Lawrence," she said, her troubled gaze lifting to his, "please hear me out."

Frustrated, he opened his mouth to speak, then closed it and nodded, his eyes never leaving her face.

"Perhaps if things had been different. If–if certain things hadn't happened. . .perhaps then. . ."

Lawrence straightened in his chair as understanding dawned. "This is about what happened to your father, isn't it?"

Annabelle hesitated, then nodded slightly. "Yes," she said in a soft whisper, barely heard above the stringed instruments.

"Annabelle, I don't care about that!" At her look of hurt surprise, he hastily inserted, "I mean, I care that you were victimized and that you lost your house, of course, but all of that has no effect on the way I feel about you—"

"Lawrence," she interrupted, raising a hand. "Please don't say anything else. I've thought long and hard about this, and I've decided it's the best thing for both of us."

"Oh, really," Lawrence said a bit sarcastically. "You decided, did you?"

"Yes. Considering your former relationship with Frances. . ."

"What does Frances have to do with us?"

She looked down and bit the inside of her lip until she tasted blood.

"Annabelle?"

"Lawrence, don't you see? If our relationship was to deepen. . .and we were to marry one day. . ." She broke off momentarily, her cheeks growing uncomfortably hot. She knew she really was assuming a great deal since he'd never told her he loved her. But she had to make him see the truth. She forced herself to continue. "Then you would always wonder if I were only interested in you for your wealth, like–like Frances was."

"Annabelle, I—"

"It's true," she insisted. "Maybe you wouldn't feel that way at the beginning. But one day you would start to wonder, to question, to regret the day you talked to that little girl on the staircase many years ago at the ball."

"Annabelle, this is ridiculous. . . ."

"No, it's not—you simply don't see it yet. But later, when you think about what I've said, you'll realize I'm right, that it would be better if we didn't see one another anymore," she ended on a whisper, her heart twisting in pain.

Lawrence pushed a frustrated hand through his dark locks, disturbing his impeccably groomed hair. One errant strand lay against his forehead, reminding Annabelle of the young man she'd met eight years earlier. His eyes had a pleading, almost desperate look to them that tore at her heart.

"Please understand, Lawrence," she whispered, "I could never bear for you to look at me with suspicion or derision. And now that I no longer belong to the wealthy class, it's entirely possible one day you would think I had ulterior motives. I'm certain even your family—"

"This isn't about my family!" Lawrence interrupted angrily. "This is about *us*. We've known one another too long, Annabelle, and we've shared a closeness I've never experienced with anyone else. Do you honestly think I can let you just walk out of my life?"

"We've made it through the past four years without one another. It may be hard at first, but I'm sure we'll manage," she said, picking up her spoon and stirring her coffee, though it didn't need it.

"When we were friends, we were young and innocent, not bound by propriety's demands," she continued. "Now we're adults, and the world expects more from us—from you. You're wrong if you think this has nothing to do with your family. Eventually you'll receive the title of earl and one day, perhaps, duke. The Caldwell name is well respected—many look to your family as an example. What would people say if you were to marry a penniless woman? It was different before we lost everything. At least then I had my mother's inheritance, even if I didn't have a title. But now I have nothing to give—no dowry, nothing. And I don't want you or your parents to think of me as another Frances Davenport," she said, shaking her head sadly.

"Annabelle—"

"I'm sorry, Lawrence; you'll never know how sorry." She rose from her chair, tears clouding her eyes. "There's nothing more to say except good-bye. God keep you always."

"Annabelle. . ."

Before he could say more, she turned and walked hurriedly past the other tables and out the door.

❧

Lawrence fell back in his chair, stunned. Had tonight really happened? Had she just walked out of his life?

He had been a fool to tell Annabelle about Frances—he could see that now. Of course, he'd merely been sharing a confidence with her, trusting her as she'd trusted him with her painful revelation about her ex-fiancé. He'd had no idea at the time that his words would boomerang and hit him smack in the face.

Groaning, he ran a hand over the back of his hair, his eyes going to the window and the dark Atlantic Ocean. Vaguely he noted there was no moon tonight. How fitting. The light had just fled his life as well.

The steward came to see if he wanted anything, and Lawrence almost told him to bring him a scotch from the bar, but he declined at the last moment and ordered another cup of coffee instead. Though the temptation to get roaring drunk was great, Lawrence had never done so and didn't care to start now. Besides, he needed to maintain a clear head, to think through this unexpected turn of events and decide what to do next.

He drank the black coffee, feeling as bitter as the strong brew tasted. *And to think, I was going to propose my plan tonight and tell her I love her,* he thought wryly. Suddenly he straightened, eyes going wide. He never told her he loved her! Of course, she hadn't given him much of a chance to say anything. Would it have made a difference if she'd known the extent of his feelings? Probably not. She'd been determined, stubborn, insistent, impossible. . .and oh, so beautiful.

Very well, then. Lawrence would leave her to her solitude tonight and give himself time to think, time to invent a believable argument opposing her ridiculous claims—one that she couldn't possibly refute. He would make her see the truth, and then he would tell her of his love for her.

Tomorrow morning Lawrence would execute his plan at the first opportunity that presented itself. He would seek her out and have his say—even if he had to tie the beautiful, independent Miss Annabelle Mooreland to a chair until he finished speaking what was on his mind.

The likelihood of him executing such a stunt was slim; still, the thought brought a grin to his lips, and, hopeful again, Lawrence finished his coffee and left the Palm Room.

fourteen

Tearfully, Annabelle hurried down the hallway, half hoping Lawrence would come after her. He didn't. *Of course, it's better this way,* she told her traitorous heart. *Better to end it all neatly and not prolong the pain.*

Annabelle descended the grand staircase, hoping she wouldn't run into Eric again. Upon reaching B-deck, she practically flew down the carpeted corridor and hurried to her room. Once inside, Annabelle relaxed, and then the tears came in earnest. She threw herself on her bed and cried for all that might have been with Lawrence.

After a few minutes, when the torrent had subsided, she sat up and wiped her eyes. Strangely, she felt somewhat better, though her heart still lay like a heavy stone within her breast. Seeing her Bible lying on the table and remembering her vow after the church service to spend time in it, Annabelle sheepishly walked to the chair and sat down. After turning the pages to where she'd left off, she began to read the Ninety-first Psalm and felt a sudden strong desire to memorize its verses.

❧

Lawrence sat in his cabin and stared at the four paneled walls. He prayed to the Lord for wisdom and mentally rehearsed what he would say to Annabelle in the morning. Sighing, he rose from his chair, slowly stretched his arms high above him, then rolled his head to remove the kinks in his neck.

For the past couple of hours he'd required solitude. But now, even though a glance at his pocket watch showed him it was fast approaching eleven-thirty, he desired company. Perhaps he would visit the smoke room and see if any of the other gentlemen with whom he'd acquainted himself were also playing the part of a night owl. He grabbed his jacket and shrugged into it, then looking into the mirror, he adjusted his tie and used the twin brushes on his hair. Satisfied, he grabbed his coat as an afterthought and left the room, hurrying along the corridor.

Upon entering the dimly lit smoke room, Lawrence was surprised to see quite a number of men there, most of them playing cards and smoking cigars at the green felt-covered tables. And there alone in one corner, smoking his pipe, sat Edward Mooreland. The older gentleman motioned for Lawrence to join him and greeted him fondly. Once he'd sat down, Edward came straight to the point. "Well, how did it go with my daughter?"

Lawrence started, not expecting such a blunt approach, but quickly recovered. "Not well, I'm afraid, but tomorrow I will try again." At Edward's puzzled look, Lawrence explained, "I was hardly able to get a word in edgewise. Tomorrow she'll have to listen to me, though!"

Edward's eyes twinkled and he gave a deep chuckle. "She's more like her mother every day." He grew a little wistful as he stared into space, then abruptly he shook his head. "Never mind. I warned you, my boy. Annabelle has a mind of her own. She's always been rather independent, as you know. But if you want the truth. . ."

A slight jarring sensation made the tea in Edward's cup slosh over onto the saucer; puzzled, he broke off in midsentence, looking down at it.

"Hey, boys, we've just grazed an iceberg!" a loud voice called into the room a few seconds later. Lawrence shared a look with Edward. Upon seeing a few men rush outside to the promenade deck, the two rose and followed them.

It was incredibly cold. However, no matter how hard they studied the still ocean, both toward the bow and stern, they couldn't see anything. Lawrence looked long and hard, but it was no use. He returned to the smoke room, a bit disappointed.

He would like to have seen an iceberg, never having seen one before. Oh, well, perhaps tomorrow he'd get another chance. He'd heard there'd been recent sightings.

They returned to their table, and Edward ordered another tea, his having gone cold from sitting too long. Lawrence was relieved to note that Edward wasn't drinking an alcoholic beverage tonight. Not since the evening of the fateful card game had Lawrence seen a drink in Edward's hand.

Suddenly all was quiet as the ship came to a complete halt.

The men looked at one another, puzzled. There was silence in the room, a silence never before experienced on the ship, and several of the men again left the tables to investigate the strange occurrence.

Lawrence wasn't certain how much time elapsed, but soon the *Titanic* began to slowly move forward again, but very slowly. He leaned back in his chair, relieved the problem had been fixed. However, his relief was short-lived. Once again the mighty ocean liner stopped and sat still and silent on the calm sea.

"I don't like this one bit, Lord Caldwell."

"I'm certain there's no cause for alarm," Lawrence said, trying to reassure the older man. But he too felt a strange unease.

"I'm going below to check on Annabelle."

"If you don't mind, Mr. Mooreland, I'd like to come with you," Lawrence said. Edward nodded and the two men left.

❧

Annabelle sat up, wondering what had jolted her awake. . .an impact of some sort. Puzzled, she rushed to the porthole and turned her head from side to side to look. A dark, craggy form toward the stern drifted away as the boat passed it. However, the night was pitch black and Annabelle couldn't really tell what it was.

Curious but not alarmed, she closed her Bible, which she'd been reading before nodding off. She was still dressed in her evening clothes, though it was probably quite late—she felt as though she'd been asleep for a long time. When Sadie came to Annabelle's room earlier to help her get ready for bed, Annabelle had waved her off, too intent in the Psalm she was reading. It dealt with how God had rescued David in a time of great trouble.

Suddenly an eerie silence filled the room as the boat stopped moving. Now more than a little curious, Annabelle walked to the door, grateful she was still dressed, and looked out into the corridor. Several other passengers left their rooms, everyone asking one another what had happened. Most were still in nightdress with wrappers tightly wrapped around them. A small child began to cry. "Hush, Ida, it's all right," a mother softly crooned.

Annabelle walked down the corridor, intent on finding a steward. After a moment, she spotted one.

"Miss, you should go back to your room before you catch your death of cold. There's no need for alarm—a simple malfunction. It will be fixed in no time," he promised.

Annabelle turned away, feeling reassured but tired. She decided it was high time to retire for the evening. When the boat started moving slowly forward, Annabelle breathed a sigh of relief. She reached her stateroom, pulled the pins out of her hair, and thought about Lawrence. She hadn't really been fair to him—hadn't let him say a word. And would she ever forget the pain in his eyes when she'd left him? *I wonder what he'd wanted to tell me,* she pondered. But it didn't really matter. There was nothing he could say to change her circumstances. Still, she supposed she should have let him have his say. She brushed her thick hair with long, fierce strokes.

Again the boat stopped, and all was silent. Confused, Annabelle laid down the brush. Hearing several people rush by her door, she walked to it and opened it. She looked in each direction, then left her cabin. After walking down the corridor, she found the same cabin steward she'd spoken with minutes earlier.

Recognizing her, he said, "I'd advise you to return to your

room and retrieve your life belt, miss. It seems we've struck an iceberg." Seeing her eyes widen, he hastily added, "Oh, there's no reason for alarm. The captain has asked that everyone go to the boat deck. Merely a precaution, you understand."

Annabelle nodded, though her heart skipped a beat. She reached her room and slipped into her fur coat, then grabbed the bulky life belt out of the closet and slung it over one arm, letting it dangle. *Merely a precaution,* she told herself. *He said it was merely a precaution.*

Annabelle hurried from her stateroom toward her father's room. After knocking at his door and receiving no answer, she paused, then tried again. She turned the knob and opened the door, peeking inside. The room was empty. Obviously he was already on the boat deck. They must have missed each other when she went in search of the steward. Oh, well, no matter. She would find him.

She descended the grand staircase, deciding she would first go to the lower deck and wake Sadie, if she wasn't already awake. However, as she passed Charlotte's door, Annabelle paused, uncertain, then lifted her hand and knocked loudly. When she received no answer, she tried once more. Thinking Charlotte had already left, she turned to leave. The door slowly swung open. Annabelle turned to the French woman to relate what the steward had said, but her words died on her lips.

Charlotte stood quietly, an emerald-green wrapper wrapped tightly around her body. A terrible bruise blackened one eye, coloring the skin a dark purple, and her lower lip was swollen to about twice its normal size.

Annabelle forgot about her mission, her eyes opening wide. "What happened to you, Charlotte? Who did this to you?"

She shook her head, as if to dismiss Annabelle's words. "It–it's nothing. I ran into a door. A foolish mistake."

Annabelle eyed her critically, doubting her words. But she knew it wasn't any of her business. "The captain has asked everyone to bring their life belt and go to the boat deck. The steward says it's nothing to be concerned about—merely a precaution. I–I just wanted you to know," Annabelle finished, suddenly uncomfortable.

"Thank you, Miss Mooreland. It was kind of you to tell me." She hesitated and opened her mouth as if she wanted to say something more, then quickly closed it. Saying another soft "thank you," she closed the door.

Annabelle paused a moment, wondering. She turned away and walked toward the grand staircase in search of Sadie. As she descended the stairs, it suddenly hit her.

Charlotte had lost her French accent.

❧

Edward and Lawrence walked hurriedly down the corridor as several people wearing their life belts rushed past them. When Edward knocked on Annabelle's door, no one answered. Seeing the door slightly ajar, he pushed it open and stepped into the room while Lawrence stayed discreetly in the hallway.

He returned quickly. "She's not here. Her life belt's missing from the closet; she's probably gone up to the boat deck along with everyone else. If we split up, we have more chance of finding her. However, I'd advise you to first go to your room and retrieve your own life belt, Lord Caldwell."

Lawrence nodded reluctantly, and the two men took off in opposite directions. Lawrence ascended the stairs, overhearing two men conversing in front of him. "The foredeck is littered with it. The steerage passengers are having a grand time tossing it at one another. Keep it as a souvenir," one of the men joked, handing the other man something.

Lawrence curiously looked over their heads to see what the man was holding. It was a piece of ice.

"What do you think about it all, Stewart?" Lawrence heard the other man ask.

"I don't know what to think really. A bit of a nuisance, certainly. I'm going to my stateroom and pack my bag. Doubtless we'll be transferred to another ship close by. I heard William say the squash racquet court on F-deck was flooding with sea water. Said it was over his shoes when he went down there a few minutes ago. And the mailroom is flooded as well. The postal clerks have been kept busy moving two hundred bags of mail from the sorting room on G-deck to a drier place. . . ."

A pang of alarm raced through Lawrence. What *did* this mean? The *Titanic* was supposed to be unsinkable! He stepped up his pace, searching for Annabelle.

❧

Annabelle walked down the corridor of C-deck to Sadie's room. After knocking on the door, she received no reply. Frustrated, she turned the knob to find the room empty. She shut the door. A woman came out of a stateroom a few doors down, dressed to go outside, a carpetbag in her hand.

"You lookin' for Sadie?"

"Yes."

"She left here about five minutes ago."

"Oh," Annabelle said, disappointed to have missed her. "Thank you."

"I'm headin' up to the top deck. I'd advise you to do the same. The sooner I get off this boat, the better."

"Oh, but—there isn't anything really wrong, you know," Annabelle was quick to say. "This is all merely a precaution. The steward told me."

"Then he lied or didn't know no better. I heard steam escapin' in my room and that's not normal. Mark my words, there's somethin' wrong. We struck an iceberg, you know," she threw over her shoulder as she hurried past Annabelle.

"Yes, I heard," Annabelle said softly under her breath. She moved down the corridor toward the stairs when she heard her name being screeched by a frantic voice.

"Miss Mooreland!"

Annabelle turned to see Maria running in her direction, a frightened look on her face.

"Have you seen Missy?"

"Missy?" Annabelle asked stupidly.

"Si! Si! We were almost to the boat deck, when she turned

and ran away. I could not catch her! And now I cannot find her," Maria said hysterically. A stream of rapid Spanish flowed from her mouth as her hands waved wildly in the air.

"Maria, calm down! Please! This isn't the time to lose your head. . . . Now, think," she said when Maria calmed a bit. Annabelle thought hard as well. Something suddenly occurred to her. "Did she have her dolls with her?"

Maria's brow puckered, but she shook her head. "I think she only had one. Yes, I'm sure of it!"

Annabelle sighed in relief. "Then she's probably gone back to her room to get the other one. You know how important those dolls are to her."

However, when Annabelle and Maria arrived at Missy's room they found it empty. The snow-white baby blanket Annabelle had given her for her birthday lay on the floor near the entrance.

"She had that with her, I remember," Maria said firmly. "That means she's been here."

"Yes," Annabelle said, relieved as she picked up the blanket. "And she's probably gone to the boat deck to look for you. Come, Maria, I'll help you find her." She put a hand on the Spanish woman's arm.

Maria paused a moment. "Thank you, Miss Mooreland. You are different than what I thought," she admitted, shamefaced.

Annabelle gave her a small smile, and they turned to go. As they walked down the corridor, Annabelle detected a slight tilt in the carpeted floor and wondered what it could mean.

fifteen

Lawrence walked along the port side, searching the faces of those who stood on the boat deck. Most people were calm, assured, a little perturbed—thinking this only to be an annoying inconvenience—and they patiently waited, hoping soon to be told they could return to their rooms.

Lawrence looked over the railing at the black water below. Bright yellow spots of light from the many portholes and windows along the *Titanic* shimmered on the ocean's calm surface. Was it his imagination or did they seem a bit closer to the water than before?

Hurriedly he moved from the rail and began to weave through the crowd. He vaguely noted that multimillionaire John Jacob Astor was reassuring his wife, who sat on a deck chair while her maid stood next to her and helped her to finish dressing. Under normal circumstances Lawrence might have stopped to chat; he'd made the gentleman's acquaintance on the second day of the voyage. But these were not normal circumstances.

He walked past crowds of people huddled in small groups, talking and shivering in the chill night air and waiting for the order to return to their rooms. He hurried past them all, praying to see a certain face.

❧

Annabelle walked along the starboard side of the boat, following Maria. They still hadn't found Missy.

"Miss Annabelle!" Relieved to hear a familiar voice, Annabelle turned and looked into Sadie's sparkling eyes. "I looked for you in your room, miss, but I couldn't find you," Sadie said with a grin.

"We must have just missed each other, Sadie. I looked for

you, too, but you'd already left."

The maid gave a nervous giggle and flicked her thick blond braid back over her shoulder. She wore a long black coat over her white nightgown. "This is quite a bit of excitement, isn't it, miss? I only hope I'm able to go back to sleep tonight."

Annabelle gave a small smile, thinking she could do without this particular kind of excitement. "Sadie, do you remember the little girl whose birthday party I attended? Have you seen her?"

"I don't rightly remember ever seeing her, miss." Sadie's eyes lowered to the white blanket on Annabelle's arm and her face grew solemn. "Is that the blanket?"

"Yes," Annabelle said, watching curiously as several members of the crew uncovered a few of the wooden lifeboats. Loud sounds of creaking and clanging filled the night air as one of the boats was readied and lowered over the rail with ropes and pulleys. After it had been lowered partway over the side, an officer turned to face the people. He spoke loudly to those around him, trying to be heard over the terrible noise of steam escaping from a vent on one of the huge smokestacks.

"Women and children to the boat, please. Men, stand back from the boats. Women and children first. No need for alarm, just a cautionary measure."

Many women demurred, preferring to stay with their husbands, and several men were allowed into the boat instead.

Sadie's eyes grew round as she watched an elderly gentleman move over the rail and step inside the boat suspended a great distance above the ocean. "Miss Annabelle. . .have you noticed how few lifeboats there are?"

Actually, Annabelle hadn't noticed. In her walks with Lawrence the past few days, she'd barely given them a second glance. They'd become a part of her world, there, in the background, but were hardly worth noticing. Her brow puckered as she mentally counted them, trying to remember how many she'd seen in her previous walks along the boat deck.

"I'm sure there'll be enough for everyone." But her tone wasn't very convincing.

"But, Miss Annabelle. . ." Sadie's eyes were wide and scared. "There aren't *any* in third class. This is all there is."

The women stared at one another in silence. Annabelle swallowed. "I'm certain the captain knows what he's doing, Sadie. He has a very reliable record. If you'd rather go on, I'll understand. There's really nothing to worry about. I have to find Missy and my father, and then I'll be right behind you."

"I'd rather not, miss." Sadie bit her lip, her eyes cutting to the boats one last time before turning back to Annabelle. "I–I need to find Hans first; he's working in third class tonight."

Annabelle hesitated, her first instinct to deny Sadie permission. However, one look into Sadie's pleading eyes was enough to convince Annabelle she couldn't do that. "All right, Sadie. Go find Hans. But afterward, you must come back and get into one of the lifeboats until they fix the problem."

"Yes, miss, of course. Thank you." She paused a moment, then, in a burst of uncharacteristic emotion, gave Annabelle a quick hug. "I'll see you soon, miss."

While Annabelle silently watched Sadie's departing figure hurrying toward the third-class section, a man whom she recognized as Thomas Andrews walked up to her. "Excuse me, miss. But Officer Murdoch has asked for all women and children to enter the lifeboats. Purely a precaution until the damage to the boat is rectified," he assured her.

"Thank you, but I'm looking for someone. I'll go later."

He paused, then nodded. "At least put your life belt on. It might help keep you warmer. It's rather cold tonight."

"Yes, thank you. I will," Annabelle murmured as she obediently slipped the well-padded jacket over her fur coat.

She looked up into the velvet-black sky twinkling with thousands of stars and noticed the moon was nowhere to be seen. It had hidden its face from them; but her heavenly Father hadn't done the same, of that Annabelle was certain. "Dear Lord, I need Your help right now. Please show me where Missy is," she whispered. Instantly a thought came, and she rushed away to find Maria.

❧

Lawrence continued searching the port side of the boat. With a pang of alarm, he noticed a lifeboat being lowered over the side and overheard a man speaking to his young daughters.

"You must both get into the boat and row around until the damage to the *Titanic* is repaired." He took the girls by the hand and walked with them the few steps to the lifeboat, which was now being filled. As he handed them inside, he added, "It does seem more dangerous for you to get into that boat than to remain with me here, but we must obey orders."

Lawrence looked into the boat, hoping to spot Annabelle. But she wasn't there. However, he did see the woman who'd been with Annabelle after church services. "Mrs. Brown," he called, doubting she could hear him over all the noise. He felt momentary relief when she looked up. "Have you seen Miss Mooreland?"

She shook her head, lifting her hands in a shrug, and he sighed. Well, there was still the other side of the ship. He hurried down the deck to the starboard side.

❧

"Maria!"

The Spanish woman turned, her expression hopeful. But when she saw no golden-haired child running alongside Annabelle, her face fell. Annabelle hurried to the governess, her words coming out of her mouth before she'd even stopped to catch her breath.

"Maria, I need you to show me where Missy's room is. I can't remember the number."

Maria shook her head. "We tried there already."

"No, Maria, we didn't. We only looked in the door. *We didn't search the room,*" Annabelle said, stressing each word.

A hopeful light burned in Maria's dark eyes. "*Si!* You are right! Come, I will show you."

The women hurried down the first-class companionway,

only just missing Lawrence as he rushed from the port side to the starboard side of the boat.

❧

Lawrence scanned the deck, growing anxious. *Lord, please don't let anything happen to Annabelle. Please help me find her and get her safely off this boat.* For, as he had searched, Lawrence realized the horrible truth; there weren't enough lifeboats for everyone. And the ship, the mighty *Titanic*, was going down—despite what the crew was telling the passengers, to avoid a panic, more than likely. Certainly the crewmen and officers, who made sailing the sea their life's work, must know the truth.

"Lord Caldwell!"

Hearing Edward's voice, Lawrence turned, hoping to see Annabelle beside him. But Edward stood alone.

"No luck yet?" Edward questioned gruffly, though the answer was obvious.

"No. I haven't been able to locate her."

He gave a brusque nod. "You stay up top. I'm going down below. We'll find her," Edward said and hurried off, leaving Lawrence to scour the boat deck once again.

❧

Annabelle and Maria quickly walked down the corridor of C-deck. They passed a stewardess who loudly knocked on one of the doors. As it opened, Annabelle heard her say, "Please put on your life belts and go to the boat deck. Captain's orders."

Maria threw open the door and turned on the light in the stateroom; Annabelle rushed in behind her. Maria looked in one direction and Annabelle the other. There was no sign of the missing child. Biting the inside of her lip, Annabelle scanned the room carefully and noticed an inch of material sticking out from underneath the curtained bed.

She dropped to her hands and knees, lifted the pink spread, then gave a relieved sigh. "I found her, Maria." Carefully, Annabelle pulled the sleeping child from underneath the bed. Missy groaned, clutching both dolls closer to her chest.

"Missy, wake up!" Annabelle insisted softly.

Golden eyelashes flickered, then cornflower-blue eyes opened wide and looked at her. "Miss Annabelle!" the child cried, jumping up and throwing her arms around Annabelle's neck. The dolls dropped to the carpeted floor. "I was so scared! Everybody was talking so loud, and I had to find my dolly. And then when I tried to find Maria, I got lost and came back here. I want my mommy," she sobbed against Annabelle's shoulder.

Maria knelt down and pulled the little girl close to her. "Hush, little *niña*. We will go and find your mother, *si?* She must be worried. You must never run off like that again!"

The blond head nodded up and down against Maria's chest. Maria stood, pulling Missy up with her, then looked up. "Thank you so much. . .Annabelle," she said softly, her eyes saying more than her words.

Annabelle smiled and picked up the two dolls, relieved that all had ended well.

❧

Lawrence completed his search of the starboard side with no success. People around him were beginning to look more anxious and puzzled, though there was still an outward show of calm.

The sound of stringed instruments suddenly carried over the cold night air as a band began to play a cheery, bouncy song. It provided a strange accompaniment to the noises of creaking and clanging, hissing and groaning of the dying ship, and of many lifeboats being hoisted and lowered over the side. Lawrence looked up to the top platform of the boat deck where bandmaster Wallace Hartley stood directing his seven musicians, giving a party atmosphere to the bizarre situation. Several of the passengers relaxed, and some joked with one another, smiling.

A man turned to his comrade. "If the orchestra has come up here to entertain us, certainly there could be nothing terribly wrong with the ship. It's a mere annoyance, nothing more." However, the look in his eyes belied his words.

Lawrence listened as a few men began to persuade their wives to leave them and get into the lifeboats, assuring and comforting their women, telling them, "As the officers said, it's only a precaution. I'll take another boat and meet you later."

Though several women agreed, others shook their heads, stating they would rather stay with their husbands on the steel decks of the huge liner than take a chance out on the freezing water in flimsy lifeboats. Lawrence clenched his jaw, praying he would soon find Annabelle and get her to a boat.

❧

Annabelle walked to the boat deck, Missy clutching her hand and Maria on the other side of the little girl. They brushed by a couple of gentlemen blocking the stairs, and Annabelle tried to move past them. "Excuse us, please."

The men turned and stepped aside while recommending that the women head for the lifeboats. "Merely a precaution," one of them added. Annabelle thanked the men and had taken only a few steps across the floor when she heard her name being called.

"Annabelle!"

"Father!" Annabelle dropped Missy's hand, turning at the sound of the familiar voice, and walked quickly to her father, who was rushing toward her. She received his uncharacteristic hug with pleased surprise, almost dropping the dolls she still held.

"We must get you into one of the lifeboats, dear."

Annabelle nodded, then turned back to Missy and handed her the dolls and blanket. "You be a good girl, now, and don't give Maria any more problems," she said firmly, though her eyes were gentle.

"Aren't you coming, too?" Missy whined.

"I'll come later. You go find your mother. She must be worried sick."

Missy reached up toward Annabelle, who bent down. The little girl wrapped chubby arms around Annabelle's neck and gave her a kiss on the cheek. "Thank you, Miss Annabelle."

Smiling, Annabelle briefly watched the golden head until it disappeared amid the groups of people standing in the room.

"We really need to hurry, dear."

She turned back to her father. "I'm sorry, Father. You're right, of course. We should get into one of the lifeboats until the damage is repaired. The thought doesn't give me much comfort—they're so flimsy—but it can't be helped, I suppose. Father. . .?" She trailed off, curious at the solemn expression that had come over his face. His eyes avoided hers.

"They're only letting women and children into the lifeboats."

She shook her head. "Earlier, I saw several gentlemen get into a lifeboat with no problem whatsoever. I'm certain they'll let you come, too."

"No, Annabelle. I won't be going." His voice was firm.

Her brow wrinkled. "Why not?"

"Because it's time for me to go now to be with your mother. I've made my peace with God, and I'm ready."

Uncomprehending, Annabelle blinked a couple of times as she studied him, then her eyes widened in horror. "What are you saying, Father? Everyone has told me the lifeboats are a precaution. When the damage is fixed, everyone will return to the ship. You *must* be mistaken."

Edward remembered the deadly green sea water he'd seen rushing through one of the lower levels when he'd descended the stairs in his search for Annabelle and shook his head. "No, I'm not mistaken. In view of all that's happened these past few days, I can see you've matured into a strong young woman; I believe you can handle what I'm about to tell you.

"This ship is doomed," he said, lowering his voice so those standing nearby wouldn't hear. He didn't want to start a panic.

"But—"

"You must go now, Annabelle," he insisted gruffly. "You have your whole life ahead of you. My life hasn't been the same since your mother died; I want to go and be with her.

Please, Annabelle, don't make this harder on me. Release me."

Tears clouded her eyes, causing his face to swim before her. What was he saying? Could it be true? Was the ship really going down? But it was unsinkable! And yet, looking into her father's eyes, Annabelle saw the truth written there.

How could she leave him to remain behind—how could he ask this of her? True, she'd known he hadn't been happy, but she didn't want him to die, especially now that the breach was so recently healed between them! But at the same time, she was proud of his courage in the face of death. She swiped her tears away, praying for strength to do what he asked. Standing on tiptoe, she kissed his cheek. "Yes, My Papa. I release you," she choked. But she hoped it wouldn't come to that and that another ship would arrive soon so everyone would be saved.

Her father held her close for a moment and kissed her cheek, his own eyes glistening with unshed tears; then he took her elbow and hurried her along. "You must live with your aunt for a time—only for a few years. After you turn twenty-one, you'll be entitled to your trust fund."

She stopped and shook her head, dazed from his words, certain she hadn't heard him correctly. "Trust fund?"

He hesitated, looking at the stairs as if he wanted to push her up them. "Your grandparents set up a trust fund for you in America when you were born—didn't I ever tell you? It's a good thing, in light of what's happened to the house. There's still some money in the account as well—enough to take care of you for a little while. But the trust is a sizable amount; it will take care of you for many years to come. Now, Annabelle, we really must get you into a lifeboat," he insisted.

Annabelle, feeling as if she'd been transported into some bizarre dream, allowed her father to practically pull her up the stairs, her sluggish brain trying to sort through this new set of startling facts. She had a trust fund. . .the *Titanic* was sinking. . .she may never see her father again. . . .

She remembered the few lifeboats; the call for women and

children first; the order for men to stand back. Her eyes opened wide in sudden understanding as the mists moved away from her mind.

"Father, I must find Lawrence first! Please!" She tugged on his sleeve. "I have to see him!"

"He's looking for you on the boat deck. Come along, dear. We really must hurry."

sixteen

Lawrence hurried to the port side of the ship, beginning to feel as though he was walking in never-ending circles. Where was she? How would he ever find her in this swarming sea of humanity? He nervously pushed a shaking hand through his hair and approached one of the lifeboats being boarded. Instantly an officer blocked his way.

"I'll have to ask you to stand back, sir. Only women and children allowed."

"I know. I'm looking for someone; I wanted to see if she might be in the boat," Lawrence explained calmly, though his patience had worn wafer thin.

The officer looked a bit uncertain, then nodded. "You can stand there, sir, but come no closer."

Lawrence nodded and quickly scanned the fearful faces in the boat. Some of the women had blankets over their heads and were shivering from the cold, but not one of them looked back at him with beautiful emerald eyes.

As he stood there, Mrs. Straus walked up with her maid. She reached the boat, then stopped, shaking her head firmly. "I will not be separated from my husband. As we have lived together, so we will die together," she told the officer in charge. She walked over to where her husband stood and looked up at him. Lawrence barely heard her next words. "We have lived together for many years. Where you go, I will go."

Several other gentlemen, one Lawrence recognized as Colonel Gracie, tried to persuade her to change her mind, but she refused, shaking her head. Mr. Straus gently took her arm and the couple moved toward two deck chairs and sat down.

Suddenly there was a commotion as someone yelled that a

group of men was trying to take over one of the lifeboats. Along with a few others, Lawrence hurried to the bow, more than a little aware of its slight downward slope. He watched from the sidelines as an officer jumped in the boat, waving a gun.

The officer yelled at the men in the boat, cursing and calling them cowards. Then he added, "I'd like to see every one of you overboard!" The anxious men hurriedly climbed out, and the officer yelled to the crowd, "Women and children into this boat!"

Worried, Lawrence turned away from the scene; Annabelle wasn't there, either. Hadn't she heard the captain's order that everyone must go to the boat deck? That was more than an hour ago.

With long strides Lawrence headed back toward the middle of the ship, wondering if he should return to the starboard side and check there again. Suddenly a loud report sounded overhead.

Looking up, Lawrence saw the black night burst into a brilliant explosion of bright, dazzling light. A well-dressed gentleman walked past Lawrence and up to a nearby officer who stood at the rail holding a pair of binoculars to his eyes. "Excuse me, sir, but if the situation isn't serious, as you've told us, then why are we firing rockets into the air?"

The officer barely glanced at the man as he pointed to a white pinpoint in the distance. "See that light? It's a ship a few miles out. We're trying to attract its attention by sending signals; we haven't been able to reach it by wireless."

Lawrence hurried away. He knew there was a lot more the officer wasn't saying. Though the crew continued to assure the passengers that the matter wasn't serious, there was a heightening sense of impending doom in the frigid night air.

Glad he'd thought to bring his fur-lined overcoat upon leaving his room, Lawrence stuffed his cold hands into the pockets and continued his search. This was hopeless. It was obvious Annabelle wasn't on the boat deck. He wished he hadn't agreed to stay up here and look; she was probably on one of the lower decks, worried and wondering where everyone was. Making the decision to go below, he turned his head toward the companionway and inhaled sharply.

Annabelle hurried in his direction, her long dark hair streaming around her, her green eyes glued to him. He stood stock-still and blinked. When he finally realized it really was Annabelle rushing toward him and not a beautiful apparition, he took off running to meet her.

"Annabelle!"

"Lawrence!" His strong arms wrapped around her, hauling her close, and she threw her arms around his neck, burrowing her head against his chest.

Neither of them noticed Edward standing several feet away. He smiled sadly at the embracing couple, shook his head, then turned and disappeared into the crowd.

❧

"Annabelle," Lawrence breathed into her hair. "Thank God you're all right! I was so worried when I couldn't find you. . . . I didn't know what to think." She sniffled, her body trembling, and tightened her hold around him. "There's so much I want to say to you," he groaned in frustration. "I was going to speak with you tomorrow. . . . I was going to make you listen to me!"

She looked up at him, her eyes shimmering. At that moment another distress rocket burst into the starry night sky, casting brilliant white light over her face. "Tell me, Lawrence. Tell me now," she whispered.

"Oh, Annabelle," he said, his gaze moving lovingly over her features. "There isn't time. We must find you a lifeboat."

"We have all the time in the world," she insisted softly. "We have right now, this moment. This is our tomorrow." She lifted her hands to either side of his face, cradling it. "Tell me, Lawrence. Please tell me what I never gave you the chance to say a few hours ago."

He looked deeply into her eyes. For a few moments, time

was suspended and there was no danger, no sinking ship, no people hurrying past. There was only the two of them.

"I love you, Annabelle," he breathed. "I love you."

He pulled her close and his mouth descended to hers as, gently, slowly, his lips moved over her lips, reveling in their warmth, their softness. He tasted the saltiness of her tears, and his heart lurched in pain.

His mouth moved to her temple. "I've received your father's permission to court you, and I hope one day to ask you to marry me," Lawrence breathed next to her ear. "And you're wrong about my family—they love you like the daughter they never had and would welcome you with open arms, even if you were poor as a church mouse. . . . I don't care about titles or dowries, Annabelle. I only want you to be my wife. And nothing you could say will ever change that."

His voice cracked with emotion, in spite of his desire to remain calm. He closed his eyes briefly as he tried to control himself and keep up the pretense that nothing was seriously wrong. She must have no cause to suspect the imminent danger.

"And do you want to know what I would say if you asked me, Lawrence?" Annabelle pulled away to look at him. At his hesitant nod, she replied, "I would say: 'I, Annabelle Christine Guinevere Mooreland, wilt take thee, Lawrence Caldwell, to be my lawfully wedded husband; to have and to hold from this day forward; for better, for worse; for richer, for poorer; in sickness and in health; to love and to cherish; forsaking all others, as long as we both shall live.' "

Tears glistened in his eyes, making them radiate with warmth, and a sad sort of smile touched his lips. "And if the blessed day should ever come when you stand beside me as my bride, Annabelle, it would give me great pleasure to reply: 'I, Lawrence Lancelot Caldwell, do take thee, Annabelle Christine Guinevere Mooreland, to be my lawfully wedded wife; to have and to hold from this day forward; for better, for worse; for richer, for poorer; in sickness and in health; to love and to cherish; forsaking all others, I plight unto thee my troth.' "

"Lancelot and Guinevere," she breathed, eyes wide in understanding. "I never knew your middle name was Lancelot. . . . That's why you acted so strangely when I told you my full name."

Lawrence nodded, swallowing hard. "Like the story of Camelot I read to you years ago underneath the apple tree. Do you remember, Annabelle? All the time I read to you, I never dreamed I was reading to the girl who would one day be my Guinevere."

"I always wanted you for my Lancelot, even then, but I never believed it could really happen," she managed, trying not to cry. "Oh, Lawrence—I was a fool to say what I did when we talked earlier! Please forgive me. At the time I thought I was doing you a favor. . . . You're the only one I've ever loved. When I was a child you were my best friend, my hero. And as the years passed you became so much more."

Swallowing convulsively, he pulled the signet ring off his finger, then took her hand, lifting it. Carefully he slipped the gold ring onto her finger and closed her hand in a fist so it wouldn't fall off. "Keep this for me, Annabelle, until I can get you another. And know you will forever have my love. . .'til the end of time."

Her gaze flicked down to her hand, clasped tightly in both of his, and the ring, which bore his family crest. "Oh, Lawrence," she murmured, her voice trembling.

"Shhh." He placed two fingers against her lips. "Mustn't cry, Little Belle."

She barely nodded. His fingers moved to brush away the tears trickling down her cheeks, then he gently drew her to him and held her close one last time. "We have to find a lifeboat for you now," he said, trying to inject a casual air into his voice, though emotion threatened to choke it off. Reluctantly he pulled away and took her arm, but she refused to budge.

"No, Lawrence. I want to stay here with you."

He looked away from her, toward the bow of the ship. "Annabelle, we'll only be apart for a short time, I'm certain. I'll follow in another boat, after all the women and children—"

"Look at me," she interrupted. "Look at me and say that. Promise me you'll come later, Lawrence."

His eyes briefly closed; he knew she would see the truth there and knew that she must not. Yet he couldn't bring himself to lie to her, even if it was for her own good.

She spoke very softly, so softly that he almost couldn't hear her. "I know the truth. I know this isn't merely a precaution as they've told us. I know the ship is going down and there aren't enough lifeboats for everyone. I also know they're allowing only women and children onto those boats—and there aren't enough even for them."

He turned his head and looked at her sharply, anticipating what she was about to say. "Annabelle, I want you to go now," he ordered, his voice low but firm.

"No, Lawrence, I won't," she cried, the tears starting again. "I don't want to go without you! I love you so much!"

Briefly he closed his eyes, pain flickering over his features. "Oh, my beautiful, independent, stubborn Little Belle. What am I to do with you?" he murmured, his hands going to either side of her face, his fingers tangling in her long, dark hair.

"Please, let me stay," she begged, even now seeing the denial in his eyes.

"No, my love," he whispered. "No."

"But I don't want to live without you!"

His eyes searched hers, begging her to understand. "If this is my appointed time to leave this world, I could never die content, knowing your life wasn't spared. And if I don't make it—remember, my darling, we'll meet again. One day in the heavenly kingdom, we'll be together again."

His head lowered while he spoke. As he breathed the last word, his lips touched hers in a kiss—gently at first, then with more passion. They clung ever tighter, trying to make up for what they were about to lose. With painful clarity, they both realized there would probably never be another shared tomorrow.

A third distress rocket fired into the black, star-studded sky, temporarily flooding it with light and showering a dazzling glow over the couple locked in tight embrace. They were oblivious to the people running past—shouting, crying, beginning to realize this was no mere precaution as they'd been told.

Reluctantly, Lawrence broke away. "Come, darling. Before it's too late."

Annabelle tightly clutched Lawrence's arm as they moved down the crowded deck toward the lifeboat. She tried to walk slowly, wanting to prolong their last moments together, but he was determined and hurried her along, almost at a trot.

Could it be that her long-held crystalline dream of shared love between them had finally come to fulfillment. . .only to be smashed to smithereens all around her? She didn't want to be separated from him, never to see him again! She didn't want to live without Lawrence, without his friendship and his love; how had she ever thought she could? *God, where are You?! How can You let this happen to me? To us?*

Annabelle watched, horrified, as several men ahead of them, upon realizing their hopeless plight, jumped over the rail into the cold ocean below. They landed with a splash of white foam within a few feet of each other and set out swimming, obviously hoping to reach one of the lifeboats rowing away into the dark night. As Annabelle looked down, she noted with alarm that the ocean was much closer than before, and there were other heads bobbing in the freezing water.

All too soon they reached the lifeboat. An officer caught sight of Annabelle and motioned her over. "Quickly please, miss! There's room for one more."

Annabelle looked at Lawrence, her eyes wide and pleading, begging him to reconsider. But he only shook his head and delivered one last soft kiss to her lips. "Good-bye, my love," he whispered hoarsely. "It's time for you to go now."

She was tempted to refuse—to have her way and stay with him no matter how he argued. But the loving plea she read in his eyes curbed her selfish desire, and she realized just how important it was to him that she enter the lifeboat. She knew she must, no matter how it tore her apart to leave his side.

Heedless of the people who stood near, Annabelle threw her arms around his neck and kissed him hard, wanting to imprint his lips on hers, to remember their soft warmth in the cold future that lay ahead of her.

A few bittersweet seconds passed until Lawrence gently removed her arms from around his neck and broke away, hating the anguished look in her eyes but knowing his own expression mirrored hers. "You must go now," he whispered. "Hurry, my love. Pray for me, and remember the Psalms." He wiped another tear from her cheek. "Don't be sad, Little Belle; I promise we'll be together again one day. And in case I don't. . ." He broke off and swallowed hard. "Tell Mother and Father I love them."

Annabelle barely nodded as she looked up at him through her tears, trying to memorize every line of his handsome face, every feature, every expression, in the few seconds left before she must board the boat. Vaguely she heard the officer behind her urge her to hurry.

"Yes, Lawrence. I'll tell them. And you're right—we *will* be together again one day soon, darling. I love you, my Lancelot. I always have. . .and I always will," she added in a whisper. Hand shaking, she touched his lips with her fingertips and looked once more into his beautiful ice-blue eyes. She forced herself to turn away then, unwilling to say the dreaded word "Good-bye."

The officer hurriedly helped her over the rail and into the boat. She sat on the hard, narrow bench beside a woman who also was crying.

Annabelle lifted her head and spotted Lawrence through

her tears. He stood next to the rail, his eyes glued to her. She kept her gaze fixed on him as the boat lowered past A-deck, where desperate people tried to lunge into the boat through the windowless openings, only to be held at bay by an officer who waved his gun at them.

The whole evening seemed like a bizarre nightmare, making no sense at all. This couldn't be happening; the *Titanic* was unsinkable! Any minute now, Annabelle would surely wake from this horrible dream and find that she was lying on her bed in her stateroom. She would breakfast with her father and Lawrence; then she and Lawrence would stroll along the promenade, talking about all sorts of things, sharing fond memories, and discussing the Scriptures like they often did. . . .

The boat slammed onto the water with a slapping splash, breaking into her thoughts and convincing Annabelle this was no dream. A nightmare, yes. . .but no dream.

As the lifeboat moved away from the doomed ship, Annabelle felt as if her heart had been wrenched from within her to remain behind on the *Titanic* with Lawrence. "God, please help him," she whispered into the dark night. "Please, please keep him safe."

seventeen

Another distress rocket lit the air, causing Lawrence to pull his gaze away from the departing lifeboat carrying away the woman he loved. At least she would be safe.

He moved away from the rail, and instantly a man Lawrence recognized as Thomas Andrews hurried up to him. "Please, sir, where's your life belt? I must insist that you put it on!"

"I left it in my stateroom on C-deck," Lawrence murmured, still emotionally numb; he was unable to see the alarm in the other man's eyes.

"I'll try and find you another," Andrews hastily said, and within minutes, he was back with a life belt for Lawrence.

Lawrence thanked him and automatically shrugged into it, vaguely aware as Andrews moved down the deck encouraging others to do the same. But there was little need of that now. The passengers had at last realized the hopeless situation, and the majority of them needed no coercion to put on the padded jackets.

A thought came to Lawrence's mind. Where was Edward? Lawrence must find him and tell him that he'd found Annabelle and she was safe. Should he have looked for Edward and let the man say good-bye to his daughter before she'd left?

Lawrence looked around the crowded deck filled with panicked people and noticed how few lifeboats remained. Pistol shots sounded as one of the officers shot his gun into the air in a desperate attempt to hold back the milling, wild-eyed throng of men seeking escape in one of the lifeboats.

"Women and children only!" the officer screamed. "Stand back, the lot of you!"

Lawrence hurried to the companionway in search of

Edward. As he walked down the grand staircase to the next level, he saw Benjamin Guggenheim. He was dressed in a silk top hat, black tails, and white gloves, his valet next to him. Benjamin spoke to a nearby steward. "We've dressed and are prepared to go down like gentlemen. Tell my wife that I played the game straight to the end."

Lawrence hurried past them through the crowded room, searching the anxious sea of faces. He walked through the lounge, past the other stairway, and on into the smoking room. Edward wasn't there, but he was surprised to see Thomas Andrews standing and staring at a painting of ships on the ocean that hung over the fireplace mantel. His life belt was now discarded and lay on the floor at his feet.

"Mr. Andrews. . .?" Lawrence asked, puzzled.

Thomas turned to look at him with eyes that were infinitely sad and vacant and slowly shook his head. Even more slowly, he turned once again to stare up at the painting.

Lawrence backed out of the room, not knowing what else to do, and hurried down the staircase in search of Edward, a prayer for the mentally anguished Andrews—and for all who had been left behind—in his heart.

❧

Along with those in her boat, Annabelle numbly watched the great ship sink lower into the water. The hundreds of bright lights on the decks still above sea level made it easy to see those on board. Everywhere she looked, people were running, trying to find a way out of the trap they now knew they were in. Toward the stern, Annabelle caught sight of a blond woman in a long black coat over a white nightgown, holding tightly to the arm of a taller blond man wearing a steward's uniform.

Sadie! It had to be! They were still close, and Annabelle clearly saw that the woman wore her hair in a long braid. Annabelle tried to call out to her, but with all the noise on the ship, there was no way her maid could hear. *Oh, Sadie. Please find a lifeboat.* As Annabelle watched, the couple moved away, with the others, closer to the stern.

❧

Lawrence hurried down the staircase, noting that the ship seemed to slant even more. He rushed through the corridors calling Edward's name, then ran down another set of stairs to the next deck. What he saw froze his blood.

Several inches of green sea water flowed down the carpeted corridors and the floor next to the grand staircase. Lawrence hesitated only a moment before he stepped into the freezing water and sloshed his way down the corridors, calling out for Edward. By the time he returned to the grand staircase, the water was slowly but maliciously up to his knees.

Quickly he ascended to B-deck and heard what sounded like a small child crying. He located a small boy—no more than four years old—crouched behind a potted plant. He was dressed in a long nightshirt and coat, but his feet were bare.

"Where's your mother?" Lawrence asked softly. The boy only stared at him with wide brown eyes and cried even harder. Lawrence looked in both directions, undecided. He couldn't leave the boy here after what he'd seen on the deck below. The sea water was slowly but maliciously inching its way upward.

"There, there, lad. I won't hurt you." He lifted the boy, who clutched Lawrence's neck tightly. As Lawrence made a quick search of the corridors in a vain attempt to locate the child's parents, he noticed that the skinny child weighed next to nothing. Well, if he couldn't find the boy's mother, at least Lawrence would make certain the child was safe.

He headed toward the boat deck and stopped in his tracks. The ship was now much lower in the water, but with a pang of alarm, Lawrence noticed something else as well. Hearing a sudden commotion toward the stern, he turned his head to look.

The third-class passengers had just been released from steerage. Men, women, and children hurried toward the boat deck in hopes of escaping. But they were soon to learn the terrible truth that Lawrence had only just discovered.

All the lifeboats were gone.

❧

Everyone in Annabelle's boat watched in shock when the smokestack closest to the bow gave a terrible creak and groan as it fell with a crash to the deck. The screams from the ship could clearly be heard over the still, cold night by those who watched wide-eyed from the lifeboat.

Annabelle tightly clasped her frozen hands together, desperately hoping that soon she would wake up and find this had all been a bad dream, nothing more. Even the crewmen quieted their filthy talk and watched, unbelieving. They'd been allowed into the boat with the women on the assumption they knew how to row, which they didn't. One of them had tried, but had ended up rowing in wide circles. After a woman had hesitantly suggested he put the oar in the oarlock, he had looked surprised and muttered, "Oh, is that what that's for?"

Many of the women had taken over the job of rowing, which also helped to warm them. Nothing, though, could melt the ice encasing their hearts, as their eyes stayed glued to the *Titanic* and watched as she slowly submerged, foot by dreadful foot. Every one of them still had loved ones on board, and every one of them began to realize the truth: There weren't enough lifeboats. And, unless a ship came along soon, their loved ones were doomed to a watery grave.

"Pray for me, Annabelle. Remember the Psalms."

Lawrence's last words to her resounded through Annabelle's numbed brain, and she blinked as though she were coming out of a long, drugged sleep. Yes, she would pray. She would trust God to take care of Lawrence, as she should have done from the very beginning. Remembering the Psalm she'd memorized just a few short hours ago dealing with protection and deliverance from danger, Annabelle recited it for her loved ones on board.

❧

Lawrence tried to find another life belt for the boy, who tenaciously clung to his neck, but his search was futile. Now that the third-class passengers had been allowed to come to the top, any spare life belts had quickly been grabbed up.

Lawrence thought a moment, then decided. He set the boy down, prying his arms from around his neck. Quickly he undid his bulky life belt, all the while praying his idea would work. The boy was so thin and small. . .surely it could work.

Lawrence stooped down and placed the belt he was wearing over the boy, noting with relief that it just managed to cover them both. However, he hoped the child wouldn't smother—the opening at the neck was too small for both of them, and only part of the child's head came through. But there wasn't much he could do about that. Quickly he fastened the life belt. The boy clutched Lawrence's coat at the back and wrapped his legs around him, holding on for dear life. Lawrence straightened, his balance a bit unsteady, and prayed he would be able to swim carrying such a burden. But there was no alternative—he wouldn't leave the boy behind. Thank God he'd kept up with his physical fitness while on board. He was accustomed to hard, strenuous exercise and was certain he was about to be faced with the ultimate test of physical endurance.

Lawrence waited silently and listened to the musicians as they played the hymn "Autumn," listened to the frightened screams emanating from all over the ship, listened to the lap of icy water against the hull as it greedily waited to suck its mighty "unsinkable" victim to its dark depths. His hands gripped the rail and he waited, praying, meditating, trying to block out the sounds of terrible fear all around him, trying to remain calm and not panic, waiting until the boat had submerged another few feet.

Then, after a quick warning to the boy to hold his breath and a hasty but heartfelt prayer for protection on his lips, Lawrence wrapped his arms around the lad and jumped into the frigid ocean waters, which immediately closed over his head.

❧

Edward clutched the rail and watched as the lifeboat that carried his daughter became a white blur on a vast, dark ocean surrounded by ice floes. He had stood a distance away and sadly observed the parting scene between Lawrence and Annabelle, his heart rending at the thought that now Annabelle would have no one—except, of course, for a handful of distant uncles and a reclusive aunt who cared little about her.

Edward listened to the band play the melodic, slow strains of "Nearer My God to Thee" and looked out over the still waters, praying that God would spare Lawrence for his daughter.

A young, dark-headed lad of perhaps ten, obviously from steerage, by the looks of his worn clothes, rushed by, a terrified look on his face.

"Here, lad!" Edward called out. "Stop a moment, I say!"

The boy stopped and turned. Huge, fearful black eyes lifted to the elegantly dressed man standing at the rail, appearing to be calm and dignified, while everyone around him was in a state of panic. "You want speak with me, sir?" he asked shakily in a thick foreign accent.

The man nodded. "Where's your life belt, lad?"

"I no have one."

"You have now."

The boy watched, unbelieving, as the man unfastened his life belt and handed it to him. He was so stunned that for a moment he only stared. Shakily, he reached for it and slipped it on, crying his thanks and throwing his arms around the kind man.

Edward awkwardly patted the boy's head. "Hurry along, son. Run to the stern with the others, and God go with you."

"*Vaya con Dios*—God be with you, too, sir!" the boy managed before breaking his hold and turning to join the others for the mad rush to the stern of the boat.

"Oh, He is, son. He is," Edward said quietly as he watched the boy's retreating back. His mind on the upcoming reunion, Edward turned his peaceful face heavenward to look at the black velvet dome of sky sprinkled with thousands of diamondlike stars. . .while the cold sea water rushed under the soles of his shoes and the boat deck began to slowly submerge.

❧

In the cold, still air, those in Annabelle's lifeboat could clearly hear the musicians on the *Titanic* playing the moving hymn "Nearer My God to Thee." Then all music suddenly ceased as the boat tilted even more and the musicians could no longer stand.

The people in the lifeboat watched, horrified, yet unable to tear their eyes away from the nightmarish scene unfolding before them. The bow of the ship disappeared into the sea, and the *Titanic* steadily slipped down at an angle, its gigantic propellers slowly rising out of the water. Frantic passengers pulled themselves along her decks toward the stern, many people falling to the dark ocean below. Soon the middle of the ship disappeared beneath the surface, the bright lights beneath the dark waters giving off an eerie greenish glow.

A terrible crack rent the night air as the ship broke into two pieces. The stern slammed back onto the water, throwing several people into the freezing sea, but after a minute the section began rising steadily again.

"Dear God, there are so many, so many. . . ," the woman next to Annabelle whispered, mirroring Annabelle's horrified thoughts.

Rows of bright yellow lights all along the remaining two hundred feet of the ship made it easy to see what looked like hundreds of miniature people fighting for their lives. Many fell or jumped off the boat to the icy water below. Some slid down the deck at a terrific speed, bouncing off objects like broken dolls. Others desperately held on to the railing or anything else mounted to the decks.

There were continual screams and cries as the afterdeck slowly, steadily, rose even higher, its lights still burning brightly. Suddenly they began to flicker off and on, then they went out completely, causing all to go black. The dark stern of the ship rose even higher out of the water until it was completely vertical, a huge, thick black column standing upright against the glittering dome of sky. There was a terrible, mighty roar within the ship, easily heard by those in the lifeboat.

Annabelle watched wide-eyed, forgetting to breathe, while the *Titanic* hung suspended for almost a full minute, as if holding on, refusing to be sucked under. And then, with a powerful rush, the ship slid rapidly below the ocean waters in a terrible downward plunge and was no more.

"She's gone!" cried several women in the boat. Annabelle just stared, unheeding, at the vaporous mist above the still black water where the mighty *Titanic* had been just moments ago. It was as though a valve in her brain had been mercifully shut off and she'd watched it all without really being there.

And then the cries started. Men, women, children—all were crying for those in the lifeboats to come save them from the freezing water. Annabelle blinked as reality seeped in. "Oh, we've got to go back and help!"

"Are you crazy?" one of the crewmen snapped. "There's too many people in this boat now. If we go back, they'll swamp us."

"But we can't just let them stay there! They'll freeze!"

"We can't go back, I said. It would be suicide!"

Annabelle ignored the words of the cruel man and turned to the other women in the boat. "Those are your loved ones out there! Are we just going to leave them to die?" she cried, thinking of Lawrence and her father.

Several sided with Annabelle, but most agreed with the crewman.

"Our boat is so full already!"

"There's no room."

"If we went back and picked up even one, we'd likely tip over and sink."

Though the excuses were valid, they didn't change Annabelle's heart. Because their lifeboat was lowered toward the end, it was fuller than the ones that had left earlier. But surely there was some room; surely they could save a few. Above the hundreds of wailing voices pleading for attention, Annabelle thought she heard a child cry out to her mama, and she began to earnestly plead with the others.

"There are children out there! Oh, please, let's try," she begged. However, only a few others changed their mind. The rest, the majority, were adamant in their refusal and continued to row in the direction of the ship's light they'd spotted earlier from the deck of the *Titanic*.

Annabelle clapped her hands over her ears to drown out the desperate cries of those left behind. She prayed for every one of them, tears running down her face. She prayed for Lawrence, her father, Sadie, the men and women, the children. *Oh, dear God, the children!*

It was as though a soothing voice suddenly spoke inside her head, gently comforting her: *Annabelle, My daughter, do not fear for the little ones. Even now I am holding out My arms, ready to receive them into My loving embrace. Instead, pray for those who don't know Me, that they will open their hearts and receive Me before it's too late.*

The soft voice seemed so audible that Annabelle looked at the others to see if anyone else had heard it. But the solemn faces showed no evidence of having heard the beautiful voice.

Recognizing the call to intercede, Annabelle quietly did so and was aware of being filled by a soothing warmth, even though on the outside she shivered from the cold. She lifted her face to the twinkling pinpoints of lights and looked at the awesome beauty of the nighttime sky, almost able to imagine angels coming from above to receive those who'd died, taking them to heaven to be with the Lord. And as she prayed, the peace that passes all understanding soothed her spirit, even though she'd probably lost everyone dear to her heart.

❧

Annabelle tried several more times to convince those in the boat to go back and rescue some of the others, but she received the same answer each time: No.

Little by little the cries diminished until few were heard.

Soon all was quiet across the still, dark ocean.

Annabelle bit the inside of her lip and closed her eyes, knowing she'd done all she could. But the thought brought little comfort. Now she could easily hear the water lapping against the hull of their boat, the sloshing sound of the oars as they lifted and dipped into the ocean, and the clunk of ice floes they sometimes bumped against. And those from the other lifeboats who'd sung, or whistled, or cheered to drown out the pitiful cries, stopped their racket, knowing there was no more reason to make noise.

The woman next to Annabelle, who'd also wanted to go back, whispered, "Oh, God. What have we done? What have we done!"

Annabelle reached for her hand and clutched it hard, offering comfort and sharing pain. She hoped someone had gone back, that there was a chance her loved ones were still alive.

To Annabelle's complete shock, the blanket next to her foot began to move, and a whimper could distinctly be heard, quickly escalating into a loud cry. She reached down and, to everyone's amazement, picked up a baby who'd been protectively swaddled in the thick blanket. She drew the bundle close and began to croon and rock the little one, trying to hush the pitiful cries while drawing comfort from the child. The tiny bit of life she held relieved some of the ache in her heart, and she wrapped her arms tightly around the baby, trying to keep it warm, trying to save one life.

Everyone began to question the others around them: "Is it yours?" "Is that your baby?" But the mother couldn't be found, and in the chaos of the previous two hours, no one could remember an officer handing a baby to anyone.

Eventually, the baby cried itself to sleep again, and Annabelle sighed in relief. "How could anyone sleep through the horror of tonight?" she said sadly, mostly to herself.

"Babies can sleep through most anything. She sure is tiny," the woman next to her said as she continued to row.

"How do you know it's a girl?"

The woman shrugged. "I don't. Just a guess."

Annabelle studied the woman, who'd said little all night. Though it was very hard to see, Annabelle could make out the lines of strain and exhaustion on her face. "Would you like me to take over for a while? You can hold the baby."

The woman readily agreed, and, with only a little difficulty and a warning from one of the crewmen never to do it again, they changed places. Annabelle took the coarse handle and clumsily began to row, at first clacking against the other oars in front of her and behind. But soon she achieved a certain rhythm and proved to be more help than hindrance.

"My name's Annabelle Mooreland," she told the woman who held the baby close and put her cheek next to its face.

The woman straightened. "I'm Maude Harper," she offered.

The women exchanged little conversation after that, but a bond of sorts had been established. An hour later, when they still hadn't reached the elusive light of the ship, Maude sighed and said, "You think someone will find us soon?"

"I hope so," Annabelle replied, continuing to row. Her hands stung from the biting cold and the coarse wood, and her muscles were weary, but at least the exercise helped keep her warm.

Twice the crewmen set fire to rolled-up pieces of paper, using them as beacons in an effort to signal their whereabouts to any ships nearby. Earlier, they'd seen a strange glow in the sky, and a crewman had informed them it was the Northern Lights. Many times they rowed toward what they thought were ship's lights, but they turned out to be stars rising on the distant horizon.

As the night wore on, muscles Annabelle rarely used screamed for relief. Maude must have noticed how she had begun to lag at the oar, for she offered to trade again. Despite the crewman's curses and threats for the women to stay seated before they capsized the boat, Maude handed the baby to the woman next to her and stood, allowing Annabelle to slide down the bench in her place. Annabelle steadied Maude while she carefully took a few steps, sat down, and took over the oar once again.

"And I had to get stuck with a bunch of simple-minded women," the crewman muttered to himself.

"You weren't forced to get into the boat," a woman in front of Annabelle responded bitterly. "Our men would have taken much better care of us than you've done."

"That so? Well, here's something to keep you warm then."

The burly crewman carelessly flicked his lit cigarette in her direction. There were screams and shrieks as the red-hot cherry tip landed in her skirt and was hurriedly extinguished.

"Aw, leave 'em alone, mate," another crewman said casually, trying to relieve the awful tension in the boat that had been building since the *Titanic* sank. "The ladies have been through enough as it is."

"An' I don't need your lip either, Marley!"

The one named Marley continued rowing as he quietly said a few more words and managed to calm his irate partner. Afterward, Annabelle heard a woman on the boat turn to him.

"Mr. Marley," she said softly, "I just want you to know, I appreciate all your help. And if I come out of this alive, I plan to send a letter to the White Star Line telling them what a valuable employee they have in you."

The woman on the other side of Annabelle, who was now holding the sleeping baby, said under her breath, "It takes a crisis to find out the true character of a man."

Her words made Annabelle think of Lawrence and her father. Had they also helped others before the ship went down? Annabelle liked to think so. She also liked to think they were in one of the other lifeboats out on the ocean.

❧

The sky lightened and the stars faded away. Pink tinged the eastern horizon as the sun made ready for its appearance.

The baby, who'd been passed around throughout the night—all the women wanted to take care of it—became hungry and began to cry. All in the boat were thirsty, cold, and exhausted. However, there were no provisions in the lifeboat, and many of the women were dressed only in their nightgowns and coats and wore slippers on their feet.

Annabelle still wore her fur coat over her evening gown from the night before, and as she looked down at it in the brightening dawn, she noticed a long tear in the skirt. She slipped her hand in the pocket of her coat and felt for Lawrence's ring. It was much too loose to wear, and concerned she might lose it, she had put it away. Finding it now, she grasped it tightly in the palm of her hand for comfort. She wanted to pray, but her mind was too numb to do so. She'd had little more than four hours sleep in the past forty-eight hours.

And then on the horizon they clearly saw something: a light. . .and one below that; it was the hull of a ship. Help had come at last.

Some of the women began to cry as they rowed toward the large ship that bore the word *Carpathia* on its hull. Annabelle later remembered little of what happened afterward, except that the crying baby was hoisted up in a canvas bag that had been lowered, and Annabelle was tied to a narrow "swing" of sorts and pulled upward. Once her feet touched deck, her legs buckled, and one of the officers caught her and lifted her in his arms.

Annabelle had a vague impression of going down seemingly endless stairs and being carried through a corridor, then laid on a cot. A warm, coarse blanket was tucked around her shivering form, and she gratefully nestled into the softness of the pillow under her head. When feeling began to return to her numb body, the needlelike, hot pain was so intense she almost cried.

Emotionally, physically, and mentally exhausted, Annabelle lay on the small cot, Lawrence's name escaping her lips before she fell into a sound sleep.

eighteen

Screams and cries sounded throughout the night; so horrible were the wails that Annabelle pulled back in fear and clutched at the rough surface of the boat. As she watched, the huge ship, which blocked out most of the starlit sky, began to sink lower. Her father and Lawrence calmly stood on the deck and silently waved to her, but when she cried out for them to jump to the empty seats inside her boat, they slowly turned and walked away.

The great suction of the ship going under pulled her small lifeboat toward it with greedy watery fingers. She screamed and tried to row faster, but to no avail. Desperately she turned to those in the lifeboat with her, only to find that they'd been frozen; their hair and faces were encrusted with icicles, their eyes now vacant. She began to scream.

"Wake up, miss! Wake up!"

Annabelle's eyes fluttered open to find sunlight streaming through a porthole to the cot where she lay; a young stewardess was gently shaking her.

"Where am I?" Annabelle croaked in a raspy voice.

"You're on board the *Carpathia,* miss. You were rescued from a lifeboat."

"A lifeboat," Annabelle breathed, trying to force her brain to understand. "Yes, now I remember. The *Titanic*. . .Oh, dear God," Annabelle murmured, closing her eyes in horror.

The stewardess bit her lip. "I–I've brought you something to eat. 'Tisn't much, mind you. But there's not enough food for everyone on board. If you feel up to going to the dining room, you might be able to get some soup, though."

Annabelle looked at the plate with two pieces of brown bread slathered with butter. "Have all the lifeboats been rescued?"

"Yes, miss. Yesterday morning."

"Yesterday morning. . . ," Annabelle repeated. "What day is it?"

"Why, it's Tuesday, miss. You slept 'round the clock."

"Tuesday!" she exclaimed, sitting bolt upright; she ignored the wave of dizziness that assaulted her. She had to hurry and dress. She needed to search the boat to see if any of her loved ones were on board. Another thought immediately hit. She had no clothes, except for the torn velvet evening gown she wore. Though she was hardly presentable, she had little choice. Annabelle swung her legs over the bed, her head swimming. "I need to look for them," she muttered vaguely.

"You have to eat first," the stewardess urged. "You need the strength the food will give you to walk around the ship."

Reluctantly Annabelle agreed, and she hastily ate. Afterward, she had to admit she did feel a little better. She thanked the stewardess and hurried out of the room to start her search. Finding an officer, who asked her name and added it to a list of survivors he held in his hand, Annabelle questioned him concerning the whereabouts of her loved ones. He scanned the list for the names she gave him.

"I'm sorry, miss. But so far, no one with those names has been recorded." Seeing her distress, he quickly added, "But that doesn't mean there's no hope. I'm still adding names. I only just added yours. And there's another, besides myself, who's doing this as well."

Annabelle gave a small smile and nodded. Perhaps they hadn't had their names written in the ledger yet or the other officer had them on his list. She thanked him and hurried away, looking through all the public rooms and on the decks and studying every person, some of them huddled in blankets and many of them wearing nightclothes and wrappers.

Maude Harper, the woman in the lifeboat, was the first person Annabelle recognized. Maude told her that the baby they'd cared for had been joyfully reunited with its frantic mother, who'd somehow been separated from her child and put in another lifeboat, and Annabelle was happy for the unknown woman.

She was relieved to find Missy, frightened but in one piece, and her mother. When Annabelle asked about Maria, Doña Ortega informed her that Maria was unconscious in the officers' quarters below deck, but she would live. However, Annabelle didn't see any sign of Charlotte or Eric. Though she'd been uncomfortable around the two, she certainly didn't wish them dead! Now she felt bad for her earlier actions—especially toward Charlotte. Annabelle fervently hoped Charlotte had responded to the message of salvation Annabelle had shared with her. . .and she hoped someone had told Eric about Jesus, too. What happened Sunday night proved that no one knew when tragedy would suddenly strike and it would be too late; everyone deserved a chance to hear the message of the gospel and to make a choice.

Annabelle found the dispensary and decided to peek inside, but before she could open the door, a steward stopped her.

"You can't go in there, miss. There's two injured men inside in a state of undress. One of 'em was struck in the head with an oar when he swam to them, beggin' them to save his son. And the other is the young wireless operator, Harold Bride."

"Oh, dear. Did the boy live?" she asked.

"Aye. But the poor lad will likely be a cripple. He has severe frostbite in both feet, just like Mr. Bride does. They may have to cut off a few of the lad's toes."

"Oh, how horrible!" Annabelle's eyes went wide.

"That it is," the steward agreed. "But they're the lucky ones."

"What do you mean?" she whispered.

"Only a handful of them left in the water were rescued."

Annabelle looked at him in shock. Only a handful? But there must have been well over a thousand, from what Annabelle had seen!

"Mr. McKee," a gruff voice full of authority interrupted. "Haven't you duties to perform?"

The steward talking to Annabelle turned to the officer walking toward them. "Aye, sir."

"Then I suggest you get to them."

"Aye, sir. Right away, sir." McKee hurried away.

Annabelle put a hand to the officer's sleeve before he, too, could walk away. He turned, his bushy eyebrows raised.

"Excuse me, sir, but could you tell me. . .is it true what that steward said? Were only a few in the water rescued?" Annabelle asked, her tone pleading with him to say otherwise.

"Aye, miss. From what we've learned, it's so," he said, emotion coloring his voice.

Her heart turned into a heavy stone, threatening to block off her breathing. "Is there a chance there are more lifeboats waiting to be rescued?"

"No, miss. The last one was picked up at approximately eight-thirty yesterday morning."

"But–but maybe there are still some alive in the water, or perhaps some of the people may have climbed out onto an iceberg?" she asked hopefully.

He looked at her sadly. "We returned to the site of the sinking earlier and circled the waters. No one was found."

"Oh, my," she breathed, feeling as if she might faint.

His brows furrowed in concern. "Are you looking for someone?"

"Yes." It came out little more than a squeak.

"Perhaps they're on the boat deck in the third-class steerage section," he suggested helpfully. "In all the excitement, it's possible a mistake was made."

"Yes, thank you! I'll go and look now."

"Will you be okay?" he asked gruffly, noting her pale face.

"Yes. I'll be fine. Thank you for your help."

Annabelle hurried to the third-class section. But as she studied the huddled, dejected forms in hopes of seeing a familiar, loved face, she soon realized it was pointless. They weren't there.

She climbed the stairs and went through the gate leading

back into first class. On her way to the boat deck, she ran into Maggie Brown. The two women hugged in reunion, and Annabelle tearfully told Maggie the situation.

Maggie patted Annabelle on the back. "It'll be okay, honey. In all the excitement it's possible you mighta missed them. You oughta try again later."

Annabelle barely nodded. Maggie studied her wretched expression. "Now, now." Maggie put her arm around Annabelle's shoulders, steering her down the corridor to the dining room. "What you need is a good meal. Things'll look better soon. I'll bet you find 'em all safe and sound—snug as a bug in a rug."

Annabelle nodded, then swallowed hard. "There were so many, Maggie. So many. . ." Her voice trailed off.

"I know, honey. I know."

Later that afternoon, Annabelle again searched the decks, but to no avail. The truth was becoming clearer; Annabelle was the only one who'd survived. But still she hoped. Later, she begged one of the officers to let her look at the completed list; but none of the names Annabelle hoped to see were written there.

She went through the rest of the day in a fog similar to the one in which the *Carpathia* traveled that evening. The weather was so much different than when she'd been on the *Titanic*, but it matched the way she felt inside. The seas were choppy, the winds bitterly cold, the skies stormy. Annabelle walked the deck. Cold needles of ocean spray stung her face.

"Oh, God," she cried to the dark skies. "How can I go on without him? Why did this have to happen?" Only the sound of the sea splashing against the boat answered her sad queries.

Hot tears running down her face collided with cold drops of saltwater. She thrust her hand into her coat pocket and pulled up the ring—Lawrence's ring. " 'Til we meet again, my love. . . ," she said softly, tears choking her voice. Putting the ring to her lips, she kissed it, then carefully dropped it back into her pocket.

She would never marry. There could never be another. She

felt empty inside, drained, but she knew one thing. Like David had done in the Psalms—when his entire world was falling apart—Annabelle would simply have to trust God to be God and cling tightly to Him. She had no one else.

❧

"Excuse me, steward?" Annabelle called out to the white-jacketed man in front of her.

"Aye, miss?"

"I wanted to inquire as to how the boy in the infirmary is doing. The one with frostbite in his feet."

The steward grimaced. "Not very well, miss. Poor lad is little more than a babe, but likely he'll be a cripple for the rest of his life. And he lost his mama in the sinking, too."

"Oh, the poor thing," Annabelle said sadly.

"Likely when we reach New York and he's taken to a hospital, the doctor will have to cut off his toes."

She briefly closed her eyes, her heart hurting for the child. "I wonder, is there any way I could see him? I mean, I know his father is in there as well, and—"

"Oh, no, miss. He was released this morning, and Mr. Bride is also out of the room for the time being."

"Then may I see the boy?"

He looked uncertain. "I'll have to ask permission. Are you a relative by any chance?"

"No. Just someone who cares."

He eyed the calm woman with the beautiful emerald eyes, which were rather bloodshot from crying. Obviously she'd lost someone in the sinking. But then again, hadn't everyone? "I'll see what I can do."

"Thank you," Annabelle said sincerely. She watched him walk away. Ever since that morning, she'd felt a strong impression in her spirit to visit the child. She'd spent all day Wednesday in the officers' quarters below decks—where some of the *Titanic*'s survivors slept at night—angry, crying, pleading, and finally, accepting her sad set of circumstances. This morning, she'd gone to God, begging Him to help her and give her the desire to go on without Lawrence. Almost instantly, she remembered the boy in the infirmary and knew she must go to him.

Fifteen minutes later, upon receiving permission, Annabelle entered the room and went to the small child who lay on a cot. Both his feet were wrapped in white bandages, which were awkward-looking on his sticklike legs. She looked down at the fearful, wide eyes in the pinched, narrow face. Slowly she lifted her arm and laid a hand on the curly blond head. The boy didn't flinch but only looked at her and blinked his eyes.

"Are you an angel?" he asked in a babylike voice that trembled a little.

"No, dear."

"My mama went to be with the angels," he said, the tears coming to his brown eyes.

"I know," Annabelle said softly. "I know."

Her heart wrenching at his pain, she knelt down and gently drew him to her. His thin arms wrapped tightly around her neck, and he began to cry.

❧

After promising to visit him again soon, Annabelle left the boy and walked down the corridor to the stairs that led to the upper deck. It was strange, but an instant bond of love and friendship had sprung up between them during the short visit. *Because we've both just lost a parent?* she wondered.

Annabelle had been told they would reach the shores of America soon, so she walked up to the covered deck to look for land, even though it was evening. Thunder crashed and lightning ripped open the sky; a sheet of blinding rain obscured any view.

Dismayed, Annabelle turned to go back down below, then stopped. Several yards away, a man stood at the rail watching the spectacular storm, obviously unconcerned about being splattered by a few slanting drops of cold rain. A white bandage was tied around his head, and Annabelle wondered if he could be the boy's father. She remembered that the steward had told her he'd suffered a head injury.

She almost approached him, then stopped. Certainly it wouldn't be proper to do so, even considering the unusual circumstances. Unmarried women simply didn't talk to strange men. Annabelle turned to go, then paused and looked at his dim form again. He lifted a hand to the back of his head as if to smooth his dark hair, though it only came into contact with the bandage. There was something familiar about that gesture. . . .

Her hand went to her throat and she clutched her mother's necklace. "Lawrence," she breathed.

The man's shoulders stiffened beneath his overcoat, as though he'd actually heard her whisper above the driving rain. Annabelle briefly closed her eyes in sad resignation; she'd already searched the whole boat and had seen that Lawrence's name wasn't on the list of survivors.

The man moved away from the rail. Perhaps she should go, she thought in the split second before they faced one another. She didn't want him to think she'd been staring—which she had, but for different reasons than he might guess. But before she could turn away, the man turned to face her. At that moment lightning brightened the sky, illuminating the man's face and a remarkable pair of silvery-blue eyes. Eyes like warm ice.

"Annabelle!"

Her shoulder hit the wooden frame of the companionway as she fell against it, scarcely believing what she was seeing and hearing. Only when his strong arms went around her and his hot tears fell against her temple did Annabelle realize her Lancelot had been spared. "Lawrence!" She threw her arms around him. "You're alive! You're really and truly alive!"

His hands moved to cradle her head, his fingers tangling in her dark curls, as he pulled back a fraction. His eyes hurriedly searched her features as if to make certain she were real, then his lips lowered to her upturned face, and he feverishly kissed her forehead, her closed eyelids, her teary cheeks.

"Annabelle," he breathed, and then his mouth found hers.

Locked in his embrace, she lost all sense of time. His warm lips on hers were demanding yet gentle, anxious yet relieved. She tightly clung to him, unable to believe he was really with her and not at the bottom of the cold, dark ocean.

"Oh, my Guinevere," he murmured into her hair after he'd broken the kiss, "I thought I'd lost you. I've been looking for you ever since this morning."

"I thought you were dead. . . ." Annabelle's voice wavered, and she felt as though she might cry again. "I didn't see your name on the survivors' list, and I couldn't find you."

"The list." He briefly shut his eyes. "I never checked the list." He moved with her inside the empty companionway, where they could hear one another over the sounds of the storm.

She shook her head in confusion. "How could I have missed you? I thoroughly checked the ship for you and my father and Sadie." Her voice trembled, and fresh tears came to her eyes. "They didn't make it."

He drew her to him and held her close. "Oh, my love, my Little Belle, I'm so sorry." For a few moments all was quiet as he gently comforted her, stroking her back, kissing her hair.

She lifted her wet face to him. "It's the way Father wanted it. He told me so before I left that night. He hadn't been happy since Mother died. But at least God gave us a few days to mend our relationship. . .I'm so thankful for that. And I take comfort in the fact Sadie was with the man she loved," Annabelle managed, her voice choked with tears. "But where were you?"

He smoothed the damp, straggled hair away from her face, unable to keep his hands off her. "I've been unconscious since the rescue," he explained. "I only awakened this morning."

Annabelle's eyes widened in understanding. "Then you're the one," she breathed. "The one who saved the boy in the infirmary. But they told me it was his father."

Lawrence studied her. "You mean Peter," he said softly. "But what's this about his father? I understood he's now an orphan."

Annabelle swallowed hard. "They told me—when I wanted to search the dispensary—that a man had been injured trying to save his son. And they and Mr. Bride were the only ones in the room."

Lawrence nodded. He looked to the stormy skies beyond the open doorway. "I found Peter before the *Titanic* went down. I jumped ship with him and was able to swim to a lifeboat. I begged them to take the child, but got struck with an oar—whether accidentally or on purpose, I don't know. I don't remember much after that. . . ." His eyes closed briefly, then opened to look at her.

"I suppose I finally got the taste of adventure I've always wanted," he said dryly, though his gaze was tortured.

"Oh, Lawrence, I just thank God you were spared," Annabelle said quietly, her fingers running along his bristly cheek; she needed to touch him, still hardly able to believe he was really standing in front of her.

Lawrence frowned. "But why me? So many were left to die in the freezing waters. I suppose they took me along with the boy, since we were laced together in a life belt, but I still can't believe all those who were lost. Women and children! Why was I spared?" His eyes closed in pain.

"Stop it, Lawrence!" Her hands went to either side of his face. "It wasn't your fault that there weren't enough lifeboats—you did all you could do. God answered my prayers—you're alive!" Her emerald eyes blazed with an inner fire. "I prayed that night, just like you asked me to do. And I'm so thankful you're here now! Instead of questioning why you were spared, just be grateful you were. God gave your life back to you, Lawrence. Don't wonder why—just be thankful."

"Yes," he said after a moment. "Yes, you're right. And I intend to spend every moment I have left remembering that and helping others in my Savior's name." He looked at her strangely, as if he wanted to say something but didn't quite know how.

"Annabelle, you know I love you. Everything I told you before you left the *Titanic* that night—I meant it sincerely. I want to marry you, to make you my own."

Annabelle's eyes were bright. "And I also meant everything I said, Lawrence. I want to be your wife. The reasons I had for staying away were foolish. *I* was foolish."

"My love," he breathed. Raising her hand to his lips, he kissed the open palm gently. He lowered her hand, not letting go, and looked down into her face, his eyes solemn. "I have something to ask you, Annabelle, something very important." He paused a moment, trying to frame his words. "Do you think you could share your heart with another besides me?"

She looked puzzled, then her brow smoothed. "You mean Peter."

"Yes," Lawrence said with a nod. "He has no one, from what I've learned. His mother obviously died in the sinking, and from what he told me, his father is dead also. He doesn't know what his surname is. If no one claims him when we reach New York, I plan to adopt him. I've grown rather attached to the lad, and I don't want to see him end up in an orphanage.

"I plan to seek the services of a highly qualified doctor once we arrive in Manhattan—I only pray it's not too late to save his feet. I want to do everything I can to help ensure that he doesn't walk with crutches the rest of his life," he ended hurriedly, his words almost tripping over themselves, afraid of what Annabelle's answer would be. He didn't want to lose her, but he felt he must do what he could to help the lad.

She looked into his eyes steadily. "He's a sweet boy."

"You've seen him?" Lawrence asked in surprise.

"I just came from visiting with him before I found you," Annabelle explained. "And in the short time I was with him, he stole a little piece of my heart. I want to help you do whatever we can for Peter, even if that means only being his mother."

Tears came to Lawrence's eyes at her sincere words. "You will make a wonderful mother." His lips briefly lowered to hers. "Do you still have the ring I gave you, Annabelle?"

She nodded and pulled it out of her pocket. He took it from her and once again slid it on the third finger of her left hand. "After we reach New York," he said, "I plan to trade that for a diamond. You can give it back to me then."

"You certainly do have a great many plans, Lord Caldwell," she teased, suddenly lighthearted despite the fierce storm raging about them, despite the tragedy of the past few days. God had delivered the man she loved from a watery grave and brought him back to her arms. How could she not feel anything but happy?

He smiled, the first real smile she'd seen in a long time. "Yes, I suppose I do, Miss Mooreland. But they're all empty without you beside me to share them. . . . Thank God you were spared," he rasped, his voice again choked with emotion.

He lifted the hand with his ring to his mouth, kissing her fingers gently, his eyes locked with hers. "For as long as we both shall live, Annabelle, I promise to love you with every breath I take," he pledged softly. "This is our tomorrow, and may God give us many more besides."

"Oh, Lawrence," she breathed, unable to get anything else past the sudden lump in her throat.

He took her in his arms and kissed her, sealing his promise, while the Statue of Liberty dimly appeared on the horizon, bearing its famous motto: "Give me your tired, your poor, your huddled masses, yearning to breathe free. The wretched refuse of your teeming shore, send these the homeless, tempest-tossed to me. I lift my lamp beside the golden door."

Arm in arm, Lawrence and Annabelle looked past the stormy skies toward the bright beacon of hope standing in the harbor; toward a future together, with God's loving hand leading them along the watercourses of life; toward thousands of bright tomorrows to share side by side.

And in their hearts they thanked their Savior for making it all possible.

epilogue

Annabelle touched the diamond on her finger and smiled as she looked out the latticed window at the rolling green lawns of Fairview. It had been almost a year since she'd spoken the treasured vows in front of a minister, forever binding her to Lawrence. And God had blessed them both.

Peter, his blond curls bouncing, waved to her as he cantered past on the black pony he'd received from the earl seven months ago. Laughing softly, Annabelle waved back.

Though Peter would always need a crutch, he had learned to walk with it quite well. A skilled doctor had done all he could to help the boy, but despite his best efforts, Peter had lost two toes on his left foot. Yet the child seemed happy, wrapped up as he was in the love of his new family.

Several months after Lawrence married Annabelle, he received a wire stating that his father was ill—though his condition wasn't serious. Still, Lawrence felt the time had come to leave America. It had been difficult for Annabelle to board a ship, though she'd known all along that a return to England was inevitable. But she had secretly hoped she wouldn't have to face such an undertaking for some time.

Throughout the voyage she clung to God, trusting He would protect them as He'd done when the *Titanic* sank over a year earlier. And He did. Nevertheless, she'd been relieved when Lawrence promised she would never have to set foot on a ship again.

A mewling sound reached her ears, breaking into her reverie, and Annabelle's expression softened as she bent over the cradle and touched her infant daughter's rosy cheek. Blue eyes blinked open, and Annabelle was thrilled when a small smile appeared.

"Ah, little Gwen. You're happy to be here, too, aren't you?" she crooned, offering a finger. The baby reached for it and grasped it tightly, causing Annabelle to give a soft chuckle.

"Annabelle! What are you doing out of bed?"

Lawrence's hushed words preceded him as he quietly entered the nursery, coming up behind her. Putting gentle hands on her upper arms, he briefly looked over her shoulder at their tiny gift from heaven before turning Annabelle to face him.

"The doctor said you were to rest," he admonished, his voice soft.

"I grew weary of lying in my room." She gave a little shrug. "After all, it's been almost a week since the baby was born. I'm fine, Lawrence—really I am."

He emitted a long, drawn-out sigh. "Oh, my beautiful, independent, stubborn Little Belle. What *am* I to do with you?" he teased, shaking his head in mock frustration.

Quirking one eyebrow, she gave him a coquettish smile.

"Love me?"

He grinned, and his ice blue eyes warmed. " 'Til the end of time, darling," he murmured, drawing her close. " 'Til the end of time. . . ."

A Letter To Our Readers

Dear Reader:

In order that we might better contribute to your reading enjoyment, we would appreciate your taking a few minutes to respond to the following questions. We welcome your comments and read each form and letter we receive. When completed, please return to the following:

Rebecca Germany, Fiction Editor
Heartsong Presents
PO Box 719
Uhrichsville, Ohio 44683

1. Did you enjoy reading *'Til We Meet Again?*
   ❑ Very much. I would like to see more books by this author!
   ❑ Moderately
   I would have enjoyed it more if ________________

   ____

   ____

2. Are you a member of **Heartsong Presents**? Yes ❑ No ❑
   If no, where did you purchase this book?______________

   ____

3. How would you rate, on a scale from 1 (poor) to 5 (superior), the cover design?______________________________

4. On a scale from 1 (poor) to 10 (superior), please rate the following elements.

_____ Heroine _____ Plot

_____ Hero _____ Inspirational theme

_____ Setting _____ Secondary characters

5. These characters were special because_______________

____

____

6. How has this book inspired your life?_______________

____

____

7. What settings would you like to see covered in future **Heartsong Presents** books?_____________________

____

____

8. What are some inspirational themes you would like to see treated in future books?_____________________

____

____

9. Would you be interested in reading other **Heartsong Presents** titles? Yes ❑ No ❑

10. Please check your age range:
❑ Under 18 ❑ 18-24 ❑ 25-34
❑ 35-45 ❑ 46-55 ❑ Over 55

11. How many hours per week do you read?_______________

Name ____

Occupation ____

Address ____

City ____________________ State ___________ Zip ___________